Portia was born and raised in Melbourne, Victoria to Estonian parents who migrated to Australia after World War II. She has worked in the retail, telecommunications and real estate sectors.

She currently lives in the picturesque Gilbert Valley region, South Australia with her son, nestled between the wine growing regions of the Barossa and Clare Valleys.

She is currently working away on her next book projects, which will include the final book in her trilogy of murder mystery romance novels which started with *The Big Dead Dry*.

For my son, Miles Tyler, and dedicated to our good family friends Halina Harding and Flavella L'Amour.

Portia Stanton-Noble

PRETTY DEAD ORDINARY

AUSTIN MACAULEY PUBLISHERS™
LONDON • CAMBRIDGE • NEW YORK • SHARJAH

Copyright © Portia Stanton-Noble 2022

The right of Portia Stanton-Noble to be identified as author of this work has been asserted by the author in accordance with sections 77 and 78 of the Copyright, Designs and Patents Act 1988.

All rights reserved. No part of this publication may be reproduced, stored in a retrieval system, or transmitted in any form or by any means, electronic, mechanical, photocopying, recording, or otherwise, without the prior permission of the publishers.

Any person who commits any unauthorized act in relation to this publication may be liable to criminal prosecution and civil claims for damages.

This is a work of fiction. Names, characters, businesses, places, events, locales, and incidents are either the products of the author's imagination or used in a fictitious manner. Any resemblance to actual persons, living or dead, or actual events is purely coincidental.

A CIP catalogue record for this title is available from the British Library.

ISBN 9781398471467 (Paperback)
ISBN 9781398471474 (ePub e-book)

www.austinmacauley.com

First Published 2022
Austin Macauley Publishers Ltd®
1 Canada Square
Canary Wharf
London
E14 5AA

Chapter One

From within the walls of the solid nineteen-fifties built red brick house, a couple of voices outside exchanging some words could be barely heard above the surrounding chorus of birdsong. A car was heard driving off soon after. There was the clear sound of a pair of high heeled footsteps which echoed on concrete steps outside and then abruptly stopped. A slender pale hand unlocked and opened the painted bright lolly pink front door tentatively. The door creaked loudly but did not give way much. It needed a strong shoulder push to open it wide. She grunted and gave it her all. Finally, inside, her sensitive nose picked up the strong smell of dust and stale air in the place.

Anabella Williams had returned to the town of Brumby Flat, virtually unnoticed, dropped off by a Taxi driver from Adelaide who was very happy to get such a big fare at the beginning of the day.

She had finally come home after two long years, very much changed. Two years had passed since the infamous Brumby Flat murders. Anabella had entered a new decade of fashion style, thanks to her time spent in the correctional centre. The borrowing library there had a lot of novels and nonfiction books dating from the nineteen-sixties, which had a major impact on her need to leave the circumstances of the recent past behind.

Standing in her parents' home finally, she was comfortably dressed in a bright neon yellow shift dress and her silvery grey hair was teased high on her head, in a classic beehive style. It had not been easy to find a hairdresser who could do retro styles. It was an expensive exercise too. Her slim legs were encased in bright red tights and a pair of knee-high black leather boots with chunky heels. She still had an amazing figure for her age. She had just turned sixty-nine. Poised in her right hand, she held a small plastic yellow handbag carrying all she had brought back with her.

She walked into the adjacent dining room and stood quietly for a few moments, admiring the huge buffet full of expensive nineteen-fifties crockery. She hesitated to walk around her house any further, afraid of all the memories threatening to overwhelm her.

Standing there, she remembered the last conversation she had in that dining room, in the presence of the two city detectives. She remembered Detective Phillip Duncan asking her direct questions about her baking before delivering the shocking news.

As she recalled,

Duncan had drawn in a deep breath, "There's been a death. Apart from Bridie Browne and a homeless man, there's just been another one."

Anabella had felt her cheeks going red under her green facemask, "You mean, another murder? Is that why you're here? Oh my god."

"Yes. Sad to say but Mayor Mrs. Maggie Jarvis passed

away this afternoon. She ate a number of your cupcakes and looks like it may have caused her sudden death. We know what was in the cupcakes. I presume you know all the ingredients too."

"It was only peaches, mango, flour...oh," she had suddenly gone quiet.

"There were a couple of more interesting ingredients. Why did you want to kill Mayor Jarvis?"

"I didn't... I didn't intend to kill anyone. It has to be an accident."

"But they were your cupcakes, weren't they? I mean, you made them here, you baked them and then took them to the Raindrops shop to sell."

"Okay, okay. Someone brings me the hash. I bake them up as cookies or cupcakes, depends on what they want. They come back and just take it away. They pay me in cash. It's a cash deal, okay?"

She shook her head as if that action alone would erase the image from her memory. She walked into her original nineteen-fifties kitchen with its powder blue cupboards and black and white checkerboard lino floor. The bamboo patterned wallpaper had faded in some parts, but considering its age, it was faring quite well. She brushed a forefinger across the grey flecked laminate bench. A thick layer of dust rose into the air and settled again. Two years of dust filled her home, so she knew she had a lot of housework to catch up on.

Suddenly, her little yellow handbag started to vibrate. It took her a few seconds to register that it was her new mobile phone ringing. The correctional centre had introduced her to a number of new technologies. She had started reading a lot of newspapers, magazines, as well as the old books and using the internet. As soon as she left, she got herself a mobile phone and used it to ring one of the only two phone numbers she knew. Now, one of them was calling her back.

"Hello?" she answered it rather apprehensively. She was still wary of new technologies. She listened to the voice calmly. She nodded her head, forgetting that no one could see her.

Finally, she spoke again, "Yes, yes. I understand. I know…I'll be there. You can count on it."

The voice continued talking on the other side of the line.

"Yes, absolutely. I'm fine. I am ready to take that next step, okay?"

The voice went on.

Anabella heaved a sigh and replied, "Yes, I will meet him there. I promise you, I will. You're perfectly right. I do need to finish this. But I need some time too."

She closed the call and went on walking slowly through her home, happy to be finally free but not quite sure what to do next.

****

Raquel Willaston stared out of Phil Proctor's kitchen window at his borrowed cottage, her hazel eyes looking at nothing in particular. She was drying a handful of clean dishes with a tea towel at the sink. She was dressed in a simple V-neck black T-shirt teamed with a long pale lemon floral skirt.

More than two years had passed since she had moved into the South Australian town of Brumby Flat and her hair had grown longer, and this particular morning, she had it tied back in a sleek blond ponytail. A lot had happened since the infamous Brumby Flat murders. She had changed jobs and was now working for a major local winery, handling all their IT work. Once again, it was part time hours and it paid very well. The staff were either cellar door hands or wine makers. Their IT needs were fairly simple. They forgot passwords for their email accounts, dropped their tablets in wine vats by accident or the internet seemed to be disconnected. Which it often was because the receptionist was also in charge of paying the internet account. The young receptionist didn't always remember to pay the office bills on time. Her priority was focused on answering the phone, texting on dating apps, doing her nails and reapplying her makeup, in that order.

She sighed loudly to herself, holding a dried saucer. It had not been a great day so far. She and Phil Proctor had argued loudly over nothing important earlier that morning. She had left the house quite angry because he had won with his crazy, cool reasoning logic. She had driven to the next town to buy some groceries. On the way back, her car must have hit a sharp object on the road, as she had returned to the cottage with a flat tyre. Fortunately, a neighbour came over to deliver a misdirected parcel and he very kindly changed her tyre for her.

To make her day seem even worse, it was Proctor's day off from his latest silo painting project, but he had obviously gone out anyway. The pickup truck was gone from its prime position in the garage. Her Pontiac Firebird was always out in the elements. The duco had faded a little and some rust had appeared on the wheel arches, but she never complained to him about it.

She turned abruptly when she thought she heard the front

door open and then visibly relaxed when a familiar voice echoed down the hallway.

"Raquel, it's just me." Her very tall son Steve appeared, beaming and standing proud in his new dark navy police uniform. His thick brown hair was cut short on the sides, but a few stray curls spilled over his forehead.

Raquel let out a squeal of delight. "Oh wow, don't you look good."

"Yeah, I know. It's a great fit."

She smiled up at him, "I am so proud of you. Honestly, I didn't think you would stick at it."

He smirked, "Thanks. Hey, how are you guys doing? How's Tex going?"

It was Steve's pet nickname for Proctor and as usual, she moaned about it.

"I wish you wouldn't call him that. Well," she was about to talk in confidence to him, but they heard the front door slam shut and confident footsteps walk towards the kitchen.

Phil Proctor appeared through the doorway from the dining room, nodding his head in their direction and taking his Akubra hat off. He strode in, looking rugged yet weary in his latest western style shirt and tight stone washed jeans. He stopped for a brief moment, brushed the long fingers of his right hand through his mane of silver-grey hair and passed by Raquel without even as much as looking at her. He muttered a barely audible 'howdy' and disappeared immediately out the backdoor. He swaggered his way towards the stables, probably off to ride his borrowed black mare until sunset. He often rode alone these days.

"Oh. Righto." Steve blinked at his mother, in sympathy, "How long has this been going on?"

"Not long, but long enough. It's not the same anymore. I don't know why but we are arguing a lot. Don't take him the wrong way. He's not angry with you. I pissed him off earlier today. I don't know what to do. Maybe I have to leave him."

"Oh my god. Is old Tex cheating on you?"

"No, no. I don't see any signs of another woman involved. I think he's over me and maybe he's over Australia as well. Anyway, the spark has gone. He's nearly finished the silos now. They're looking brilliant by the way. It's his best work I reckon. So, I really think he's going to head back to New York when it's done."

She bit her bottom lip and as much as she wanted to tell her son more, she decided not to bother him with it. Otherwise, she would have told him that she and Proctor were not even sleeping together. They were sleeping in separate rooms. But that's all she would've told Steve.

If Proctor was in the mood for sex, he was no longer interested in pleasing her and just got off on his own. But two days ago, Raquel had refused his advances altogether. After that, he had become bitter, cold and remote. He hadn't talked to her since.

She turned to put the damp tea towel aside, "Anyway, I'm not going to dwell on it. I'm off to town soon to meet up with Bette and look at my bridesmaid dress. Today is the big reveal."

"That's great. I forgot your best friends' wedding's coming up. I still haven't found a date for it, you know."

"Honey, you don't need to bring someone with you. Bette will be happy just to have you there, at the wedding and the reception. Anyway, I'd better get on my way. I have to be at King William Road in two hours."

"Wow," he smirked. "That's a real posh hot spot. Her dress must be something special."

"No idea. I am about to find out. Walk out with me, honey?"

"Yeah, sure thing."

Raquel stopped for a moment at the hallway mirror, remembering that she had just a smudge of makeup on her face but then she was Bette's only bridesmaid, so it probably didn't matter. She followed her tall policeman son outside.

They parted with a big bear hug, before she climbed into her Pontiac. She had a long drive ahead of her.

She passed a succession of slow-moving road trains on the highway and as the hilly landscape flashed by, she noticed how very dry everything was. As she drove on, she only saw the odd green tree and a large patch of vineyard. Since the night of the heavy downpour when Sandy Mitchell was caught, there had only been a handful of rainy days since then. Brumby Flat was in the midst of a drought once again. It was gradually impacting the small town. If not for the thriving café section in Bette's Raindrops Shop, the doors of the business would be closed. Bette had confided in her that no umbrellas, gumboots or water skis had sold in six months. Brumby Flat's reputation as a murder town was starting to fade away, as fewer visitors were coming through. The old post office where Bridie Browne had been murdered, had since been demolished so there were no more tourists gawking at it and taking photos.

Eventually Raquel was navigating lanes of heavy city traffic. On the long drive, she had plenty of time to reflect on her relationship with Phil Proctor which didn't seem to be going anywhere.

Two hours later, Raquel arrived at King William Road, which was dotted with exclusive shops and expensive fashion boutiques. She parked in a side street. She walked down King William, reading the shop numbers. She found her destination and it was so exclusive, the bridal shop had no name, just the number in bold gold glitter lettering. She pushed the heavy double entrance doors, but they appeared to be locked. She pushed again, a bit harder this time. Still nothing happened. After a couple of minutes, she noticed an intercom on the left side of the entrance.

She pressed all the buttons and eventually a stern, terse female voice answered.

"It's not a toy. You needn't be so rough. Can we help you?"

"Yes, I am here for the bridesmaid fitting. For Bette Mitchell."

The entrance doors magically opened on their own, Raquel walked in and could see the opulence of the joint. Floor to ceiling was covered in shiny marble white tiles and there was a small row of wedding dresses on a corner rack in a far corner of the room. On the other side, there was a series of colourful bridesmaids' dresses on a neatly spaced row of shop mannequins. It was minimalism on a grand scale.

Her hazel eyes were diverted to the centre of the enormous room. Bette was there, standing on a revolving platform, admiring the puffy sleeved ivory dress with layers of chiffon swirling below her cinched in waist, in the ornate gold framed wall mirror. She caught a glimpse of her dearest friend in its' reflection and she immediately hitched up her skirts of chiffon, jumping down from the platform. The very action made the sales assistant audibly gasp and look on in horror.

Then Bette ran up to Raquel, and they embraced for a few precious seconds, squashing up the chiffon layers which brought on another gasp from the sales assistant.

When they finally released each other, Raquel exclaimed, "Wow, you look fabulous in that dress. Is this the one? Is this the dress?"

Bette smiled broadly, lightly touching her perfect shoulder length bobbed hair, "Yes doll, I love it. It's very me, don't you think?"

"Oh yeah. It's pure 'Belle of the ball' stuff. I mean, Bette of the ball."

"And I've got a little surprise too," Bette then carefully lifted down the left shoulder of the wedding dress to reveal a bloodied pad of gauze, "I want to show you my first ever and only ever tattoo. Never had one before but I felt I had something important to say."

She slowly revealed it and Raquel didn't know whether to laugh or to cry. It was in the shape of a unicorn's head featuring Bette's and Phillip's name entwined with tiny red roses.

"Isn't it great? Oh, Raquel dear. He's just the love of my life."

Raquel took a deep breath, "Well, yes, I like it, Bette. But a tattoo is forever. What if something happens, not saying anything will happen, like you fall out of love. Break up, you know? I mean, I am not saying it will happen but you're never sure of anything nowadays."

Bette looked at her darkly, "Don't you think I know when love is real? I love him, he loves me. He adores me. I know I have been waiting for Phillip Duncan to come along, into my life. I get it, doll. What's your problem with this?"

Her friend shrugged her shoulders and said with a partial smile, "Nothing. I am so happy for you. And I am so happy to share this wonderful time with you. And wow, I love your hair."

Bette patted her shoulder length hair, "Our Amy did it. It's got reverse brown streaks in it."

Her friend nodded. She recognised the look. Since Brumby Flat had doubled in size, finally they had their own mobile hairdresser. Half the ladies in town now had that same hair style with reverse brown streaks.

At that moment, the bridal shop assistant strode up to them, wringing her hands together and silently herding them into the centre of the room.

"Now. Is there anyone else coming today, Ms Mitchell?"

Bette nodded, her big blue jay eyes widening, "Oh, please call me Bette. Yes, we have to wait for my dear old school friend from Sydney, Kitty," she then turned to look at Raquel apologetically, "Now doll, you haven't met her before. I think I have talked to you about her."

Raquel looked puzzled while the shop assistant vanished from sight.

"Okay. Well, maybe not. She was a big model you know, Kitty Caulfield, in her day. 'Course it's not her real name, she was born in Russia, you know. She's appeared in a lot of the top fashion magazines. She even worked in New York for almost two days. Actually, she's still doing her modelling work I believe. She's still big in modelling but the jobs now are a bit smaller."

"Oh, I see. I thought I was the only bridesmaid," Raquel put up a hand to her make up free face.

Her friend gently took her right hand and squeezed it,

"Sorry doll, it was my darling Phil's idea," she said, "He didn't want you to feel all alone. At least you'll have another bridesmaid to talk to on the day. I know your Phil is coming along but you will be on the bridal table with us."

The shop assistant's high heel court shoes echoed across the shop floor, as she walked over to them. She seemed to come out of nowhere.

"I believe your last bridesmaid has arrived. Straight from the plane she said."

Bette grabbed up the layers of her dress and ran towards her old friend Kitty who made an entrance, just by her appearance alone. She stirred up feelings of jealousy in Raquel straight away.

Part amazon and part gazelle with long perfect legs seemingly up to her armpits, Kitty stood tall. As she walked across the floor, her long dark wavy hair billowed behind her, tugged by a wind that did not exist and she surveyed her surroundings with the palest of green eyes. Her skin was creamy and flawless, and her high cheekbones suggested her Eastern European ancestry. Her mouth was a perfect red bow and although she was wearing a shapeless, strapless cream dress with a chiffon leopard print scarf casually draped around her throat, she looked as if she had just stepped out of a fashion photo shoot. She had a brown leather satchel bag slung across her tiny chest to her hip.

Bette rushed up to hug her, but Kitty, always conscious of germs, just proffered her elegant slim right hand at a respectable arm's length. Bette looked surprised but took it and shook it furiously, "Great to see you. How long has it been, Kitty?"

Kitty cleared her long pale throat and said in a regal sounding voice which had a slight accent, "Ages, my dear, it's been ages. Ten years at least and I really thought we'd never ever meet again. Sorry, but I am a bit jetlagged."

"Wow. You just flew in from where? London? Paris? Milan?"

"Perth," she replied drily, adjusting her chiffon scarf, "I LOVE your dress, Bette. It's SO retro and so very unique looking."

"Oh yes, thank you."

Kitty didn't have the heart to tell her old friend that she looked like she was wearing a tea cosy.

She smiled just very slightly at her much shorter old friend. She had read lots of material on anti-aging prevention methods including minimal facial movements to prevent wrinkles and how to avoid bloating. The bloating part was the hardest for her. Basically, for the last two decades, she had restricted her diet to strictly champagne and strawberries at parties, mineral water and steamed vegetables at all other times. If she ate anything else, it went straight to her hips. Prone to being pear shaped, she had to avoid at least four food groups. Fortunately, champagne was okay at any time of the day.

Although Kitty told almost everyone she encountered that she had Russian aristocratic blood coursing in her veins, it wasn't entirely true. In reality, her mother was born in a small village in India and her father was a tall Hungarian gentleman. Her dark tanned skin came from her mother and her exotic good looks were a gift inherent of her father. When she was born, she had large black eyebrows but fortunately she grew into them, and her beauty blossomed as she grew taller.

She pretended her early life was one of privilege, wearing the best clothes and attending the best children's parties. It had been anything but. In reality, her parents had lived in community housing, getting along by very humble means. Fortunately, Kitty grew up with a vivid imagination. She invented her own perfect life. And she was able to convince other schoolchildren and their parents that she had servants looking after her every need and that her family lived in a grand mansion. At primary school, every parent was happy to host her overnight and wanted to desperately meet her affluent parents. But Kitty was clever, manipulative, and very imaginative. She outmanoeuvred all their best attempts. She was a confident talker and early on, she had adopted her unusual accent. She always made sure to say that her parents were far too busy socialising at charity events and the like to attend parent teacher afternoons.

Her mother was a talented dress maker and made most of Kitty's clothes out of fine silks, satins and velveteen material she purchased at sales. Kitty always looked immaculately groomed and she was taller than most of her peers, so her carefully made-up stories could be easily believed. As she got older and went to high school, she found the deception was much more difficult. After her mother suffered a nervous breakdown and couldn't hold a sewing needle still anymore, she stopped dress making altogether. Kitty had to make the rounds of op shops after school and buy second-hand dresses with good labels to keep up appearances. When friends wanted to come home and visit, she would give them an excuse. She would walk three kilometres towards the most expensive suburb if anyone watched her leave school, in case she was ever followed, then she would double back.

Academically she wasn't exceptionally bright, but she was the most popular girl in her year, every year. An average student, she did excel in languages, learning French, Japanese and German at school very easily and she even picked up some Lithuanian from her best friend as well. When she was home, she spoke a mix of Indian and Hungarian.

By the time she was sixteen, Kitty was close to being caught out. Friends were starting to ask her too many questions. But then she saw her opportunity to change her life and make the imagined one more real. A teen magazine was looking for the next top model. The prize included a modelling contract and a whole new wardrobe. She saved some money and paid for a professional photo which showed off her long dark hair, her wide green eyes framed with a dark smouldering look and her ruby red lips slightly curved in a smile. She entered the photo in the competition. The photo was a clear winner, and she was officially invited to attend the final selection evening in Sydney. It was her first experience in a plane, and she vowed she would one day fly often.

She was the tallest girl in the competition and her exotic dark looks and long slender legs impressed the judging panel. She didn't win the contract but her confidence on the catwalk and her ease posing for the camera and pushing other models out of the shot, convinced one of the judges to take her direct to another modelling agency. It wasn't long before Kitty was featured in magazines and on billboard posters. She sold top clothing labels, toothpaste, life insurance and even dog food. Her real surname was long and unpronounceable, so her agent suggested changing her name. So, when she turned eighteen, she walked into the Births, Deaths and Marriages office and walked out confidently reborn as Kitty Caulfield.

Her parents faded into the background, her mother stricken by various nervous afflictions and her Hungarian father battling arthritis from his fine work fixing broken cuckoo clocks.

Kitty's career had lasted twenty years so far, but lately she had noticed a slight decline in work assignments. In the past, she had been too busy to have a social life, and she had missed a lot of friends' weddings and birthday parties. But this time, she had accepted Bette Mitchell's wedding party invitation. She had a free space on her calendar. It was actually more of a long gap between engagements.

Bette steered her old friend towards Raquel who looked back at Kitty Caulfield with pickled lips and a frowning complexion.

"Kitty, this is my new friend Raquel Willaston, your fellow bridesmaid."

The pale slim hand came out again and Raquel shook it like a limp celery stick.

"How do you do?"

"I'm fine. Totally fine, thanks."

"Well ladies. It's time to try on your bridesmaid dresses. I imagine you're as excited, as I am."

Raquel nodded with some enthusiasm while Kitty just stared out into space over the top of her head. She was tall anyway.

The sales assistant appeared right on cue.

"This way please," she ushered them to the change rooms at the back of the showroom.

Bette settled down into the bridal throne chair, disappearing into the chiffon layers of her amazing dress. She waited eagerly to see the final results of her wedding plans coming together.

Sometimes she had to pinch herself over all the happenings over the last two years. The biggest change had been finding out her now ex-husband Sandy Mitchell was the infamous Brumby Flat serial killer. Some people in town had not forgiven her for bringing him there to wreak havoc and they largely ignored her. But Detective Phillip Duncan saved her in a number of ways, and she knew no one else would understand their relationship. Bette knew all about Duncan's missing hippy parents who had driven off in their kombi van and left him behind when he was seven years old. And Duncan had learnt that Bette's life with Sandy had not been easy. Most of the time he was very good to her but sometimes he was volatile. When he had a big mood swing, Sandy wouldn't talk to her for days.

And on top of that, on the night of the torrential rain when Sandy had tried to kill her in The Raindrops Shop, he had run over their cat. Their cat Pandora had survived a number of near-death experiences but sadly being completely flattened by a three-tonne truck and surviving that proved impossible for the resilient feline. Bette had cried for days after. Duncan was not a cat person but accepted the significance of the loss to her.

Bette smiled to herself and even blushed a little, thinking about Duncan as she waited for her bridesmaids to emerge.

The first to appear from the dressing room was Kitty, strutting out on an invisible catwalk direct to Bette. The bridesmaid dress was very plain, about knee length and of a pale pink shade, but she made it look like a million dollars. It was sleeveless and from the waist down, it was shaped like a bell. It fit her like a glove and Bette clapped her hands excitedly.

Kitty had found side pockets and thrust her slim perfect hands in them and did a perfect twirl for Bette.

Raquel followed soon after. But her entrance was much more sombre. There was no strut and certainly no twirl. She was wearing the same dress in the same colour but on her, it hung off her shoulders like it was one size too big and the bell shape did absolutely nothing for her figure. The pale pink colour against her pale skin and blond hair, did nothing for her either. And worst of all, she was well aware of it as she stood next to the perfect tanned glow of Kitty Caulfield who looked amazing in hers.

Raquel instantly burst into tears.

Bette stepped forward and gently touched her friend's forearm, "Are you okay, doll? What is it? What's wrong?" she asked in her raspy voice.

Raquel wiped away her tears, "I'm sorry Bette, but I hate it. I look terrible in this dress. It doesn't suit me."

Kitty sniffed and with hands spanning her slender waist, she said, "Get over it. You are being overly critical. I just met you five minutes ago and you're crying blue murder over a goddamn dress."

Bette frowned, "Please don't cry, doll. It's my wedding, it's going to be my big day. It's not about you or even Kitty. Sorry Kitty, but you know what I mean."

Kitty flashed her green eyes and tossed her hands up in the air, "I understand. You must know how to carry the dress. That's what they teach you in modelling. You must learn to do the same. Carry the dress and hide your distaste for it."

"I don't like the dress. I don't want to wear it."

Her friend sighed heavily and studied the tiled floor before she gave her final thoughts on the matter.

"Well, I am sorry, but I designed these dresses myself. You said to me you wanted to be a bridesmaid in my wedding. You know that it's next weekend already. If you don't like the dress, you don't have to wear it. You are not in my wedding, if that's how you really feel about it. I have to put my foot down about this, doll. I don't want my big day to be ruined."

Kitty looked smug at this point and that was enough to make up Raquel's mind.

"Okay Bette, it's okay. I won't talk about it again. This dress looks lovely really. But if you don't mind, I just want to get the shoulders nipped in a bit. Feels too loose to me and I think that will make me feel better."

"Okay. You can do that. It's at your expense, not mine."

The sales assistant suddenly rushed up in a panic.

"I hope you are taking the dress," she said firmly to Bette.

Bette knitted her eyebrows together, "Of course. I love this wedding dress."

"Oh good, because your dress is…well. You have to buy it now."

Raquel gasped when she realised what was wrong. On her friends' left shoulder where the fresh tattoo was, there was a spreading brown stain over the ivory gossamer sleeve. The gauze patch over the fresh tattoo had come loose.

Bette shook her head, "Oh no. How am I going to get that stain out?"

"It's alright. We can do that for you. I'll just add a little extra to the dress price," the shop assistant was very quick to add.

Kitty pulled a face, "Oh my god, Bette. You got yourself a tattoo. I am honestly in shock, my darling."

Bette frowned, "Well, it's not just a tattoo, Kitty. It's of me and my great love, you see."

"It's a permanent stain on your flesh, Bette. That's what it really is."

Chapter Two

She twirled around to show the stranger her best model moves. Then she giggled like a schoolgirl and sat down on the damp grass which had been watered by sprinklers earlier in the day. Kitty Caulfield was elegantly sitting cross legged and perfectly poised on the edge of the dam near to the reserve, just twenty metres away from the scene of the wedding reception which was still in full swing.

She had removed her bridesmaid dress in the ladies and underneath she had been wearing a floral slip dress which was more comfortable to wear on the hot, steamy night.

She was a perfect silhouette in the half-light reflecting from the town hall. She turned to her quiet but refined companion who was bathed in shadow and said, "Oh wow. Really? So, this dam will be extended to become part of the new housing development. To be called Brumby Hills Estate?"

They were seen to nod.

Kitty turned her head back in the direction of the hall when she heard a roar of voices.

"I have to say, this has been a really fun wedding."

She waited for an answer, but no answer came. The person in the shadows who she had spoken to, they leaned in and suddenly gripped her pale slender throat in their strong masculine hands. Kitty's pretty pale green eyes widened in fright. She tried hard to scream but the grip crushing her throat was relentless and merciless. Her hands failed at her assailant, trying hard to scratch, punch or pull her way free. But they were much stronger than her. Her assailant grunted and lifted her up by her throat and then dragged her writhing body to the waters' edge. The vice like grip continued for another long minute before the strong hands let her go and shoved her roughly down the inner, muddy walls of the dam. Her mobile phone was tossed, and followed her in.

She tumbled head over heel several times down the steep embankment and when her body hit the icy cold water, it felt like a thousand knives were stabbing at her. She struggled to breathe and keep consciousness. Caked in mud and stagnant dark water, she struggled to reach the bank. Her long fingernails scratched and scrapped the edge of its slippery, muddy surface. Trying to find something to grip on so she could pull herself up, the dam sides were too smooth and so very high. She was gasping for air and her chest was sore like hell. In the fall, she had actually broken a couple of ribs along the way down.

She tried to call out for help, but her throat was bruised from the pressure around it earlier. Her assailant had appeared to have vanished into the night. She kept trying hard to get up the sides of the dam bank but there was nothing to grip.

She kept scratching her fingernails in the mud and trying hard to scream. The water seemed to be getting colder. It seemed no one in the living world could hear her. She finally managed to say 'help' loud enough that it echoed into the warm, dark night.

Nearly a good hour had passed, and she felt exhausted. Kitty was starting to let the dam win the fight. She yelled out again but this time, she slipped under the water surface for a moment. She came gasping up for air and gave out a primal scream.

And this time she had been heard. A wedding guest casually smoking a cigarette at the edge of the dam stopped and strained to listen.

Kitty screamed out a second time.

"Hey, there's someone swimming in the dam." The guest cupped his hands together and yelled out to a group of people standing closer to the hall. But they couldn't hear him over the music. He had to run up to them to be heard.

****

Before their wedding day, Bette Mitchell was trying hard to keep up long held bridal traditions. In order to keep their love alive, she decided to ensure that Duncan kept his social distance from her that last week. They lived in the same house now, which made things a bit difficult. He was relegated to one of the upstairs bedrooms and only allowed to enter and exit by the kitchen back door. She, however, could freely use the front door and much of the house.

At Proctor's cottage, Raquel was trying to avoid her man too. For the most part, she managed it, thanks to having a busier than usual week at work. It seemed every day that week, staff were dropping their iPad in wine vats or driving their sturdy SUVs right over them.

But on the day of the wedding, Phil Proctor's presence was unavoidable. He had decided to stay home, put his feet up and was watching the tennis on television. She was rushing around getting ready, doing her hair and makeup as Bette had instructed her to do. She had steamed the bridesmaid dress and had it adjusted at the shoulders and a pinch at the waist so that it sat a bit better on her. She still didn't like the dress, but she accepted the fact she had no choice. It was all for Bette.

An hour to the wedding, Raquel was dressed and struggling with her slip-on silver glitter court shoes, when Proctor entered the bedroom. He leant his back against the wall, hands thrust in his jeans pockets and admired her.

"You're looking really good, girlie," he said, inclining his head, "When do you have to get to the church?"

"Before two o'clock. I'll make it. Easy. Now. Are you coming to the church with me?"

He smirked, "Nope. Sorry. I've been in enough weddings myself to know what the punchline is. I'll see you at the reception later, ma'am."

Raquel studied his rugged, handsome features for a moment, trying to read him.

"You were invited to the church, Phil."

He didn't say a word in response.

"Fine. I'll see you there, at the reception then," she said, her cheeks flushed red.

He casually retreated from the room, leaving her to fuss over her reflection in the mirrored robe. When she was finally happy with her image, she grabbed her car key and jumped into her Pontiac. She was at the town church by the time she blinked. Kitty was already waiting at the church doors, striking a model pose. Bette was a stickler for wedding etiquette but strangely, she didn't want to spend half the day preparing with her bridesmaids. The truth was that Bette had turned into a bridezilla. Any little thing not going the way it should, set her right off. She would explode and Duncan had copped it over the phone the day before, when there was a mix up with their honeymoon travel arrangements.

The wedding guests were starting to arrive and were gradually making their way into the church. Raquel joined Kitty at the entrance of the church, just exchanging nods with her. Kitty as usual looked immaculate and noble. Raquel was left to brush whisps of her flyaway hair off her face and lament the arrival of a new big pimple above her left nostril. She picked at it annoyingly.

Bette arrived fashionably late to church, in a large white Bentley. The bridesmaids rushed forward to assist her out of the vehicle and noticed her bristling mood. She snapped at them as she realised that on the back of her dress, the ruffles were all crumpled and wrinkled. On top of that, her makeup was starting to run as she sweltered in the multilayered dress on the hot summer's day.

Raquel shrugged her shoulders and reassured her friend, "Bette, you look amazing. You are this really gorgeous bride, and no one will notice, believe me, no one will see any imperfection."

Bette's face beamed as she entered the church entrance with renewed confidence. Her new husband was standing at the altar with the priest, waiting patiently for her. He was dressed in a new dark navy suit which fitted him perfectly, with a white carnation on his jacket lapel. He turned his head to look at her enter the church and he was not disappointed. She virtually floated down the aisle in her dress, her hair swept up in an elegant updo, holding her bouquet of local wildflowers in front of her tiny waist. It seemed the whole town of Brumby Flat had literally poured themselves into the church for the marriage of Bette to her detective.

Raquel cried a few quiet tears during the ceremony, especially at the part when the newly married couple kissed at ceremony's end. She noticed how tenderly Duncan held Bette's waist with one broad hand and held her small hand in the other as he had bent over and gently kissed her lips. She had kissed him back, making their love and marriage vows official.

The happy couple smiled for the official photographer outside the church, on the stone steps. As most of their money had gone to purchase Bette's very expensive wedding dress which included the hefty dry-cleaning bill, the Bali honeymoon and the hire car, they could only afford fifteen minutes of the wedding photographers' hourly rate. The photographer shouted out instructions like it was a model shoot and clicked madly away on their camera. Kitty was in her element and nearly stole each frame. Raquel was happy to pose only briefly with Kitty.

In their carloads, everyone headed to the local town hall for the reception. The couple had tried to put on a lavish celebration on a tight budget. Fortunately, the whole town pitched in and brought plates and trays of mainly home cooked food with them. Plates of food to share soon filled the tables.

When the beaming newlyweds arrived, their reception was already in full swing. Even the infamous town drunk had turned up. He swayed his way to the bar to grasp his prized first free boozy drink in quite some time.

Raquel had a miserable time seated at the bridal table. Kitty ended up sitting right next to the newlyweds while she was relegated to the end of the table. She tried a few times to talk to Kitty, but she was largely ignored. If she wasn't laughing along with whatever Bette said, Kitty was too busy texting away on her mobile phone. On top of that, Raquel was positioned behind a gigantic vase of flowers, but it allowed her to pick quietly away at her nose pimple. The plates of food had been distributed and she ended up with a plate of egg, salmon and dill sandwiches to graze on. As wedding guests chatted with the newlyweds and took photos of the smiling bridal party at the table, she was barely visible and made little attempt to look happy, even for her best friend.

And things seemed to get worse as the evening wore on. Kitty Caulfield had been asked to give the bridesmaid speech to the couple, and her stories talked about their old days in Sydney which Raquel knew nothing about. Everybody laughed along with her. Kitty not only had model good looks, but she also proved she had a killer sense of humour too. The serious side also came out. At one point, she turned her head and acknowledging Bette, she said, "It's a great pity that Mandy-Jane can't be here with us today to share your joy. Hey, remember Bette? At high school, they used to call us a trio of babes, because whenever we got together, we were trouble."

Bette fought back her tears and quietly nodded. Duncan put his arm gently around his wife, comforting her. He seemed to know the background story.

After Kitty's moving speech, Bette and Duncan had to perform the bridal dance. Duncan looked uncomfortable at first, as he took Bette's small hands into his. They glided beautifully over the dance hall floor to a traditional waltz. The ruffles of Bette's dress seemed to float in slow motion. At the end of it, Duncan dipped Bette elegantly to the floor and swept her up with ease in his arms. They kissed briefly and the guests clapped their approval wildly and whistled loudly.

After that, the lady DJ started to deliver dance hit after dance hit. Peering around the vase, Raquel saw Phil Proctor arrive. He swaggered into the hall, hands on hips, standing tall and noble in his best denim shirt and stone washed denim jeans. He had the uncanny ability to carry off double denim with dignity. Instead of an Akubra, he was wearing the smart white Stetson hat he had arrived in Australia with. He had added his authentic Texas belt and his old faithful pair of cowboy boots. It seemed all the women in the room had turned around to gawk at him. The single girls, the wives and the widows, all their eyes devoured his tall Texan bred and born frame. He took his time to smile at them all and dipped his hat to them. He walked confidently across the dancefloor, brushing shoulders with some of the dancing women as he passed. They smiled back at him. No one seemed upset by his touch.

Across the floor, he stopped at the bar and ordered himself a beer. Proctor stood at the bar, clutching a stubby in his hand until the country music started. He downed the beer and entered the dance floor. He joined the line dance, but it quickly evolved into something more intense when two young women came up either side of him, grinding their wide hips against him. He tipped his hat and took the hand of each lady. He ended up twirling them away one on each hand, bringing them forward and then letting them spin around him. He never missed a beat. Once again, every woman in the room seemed to be staring at him. He was smiling broadly and having a great time. Raquel was envious and sulked quietly behind the vase.

When Proctor finally sat down at the next long table, Raquel rose to go and join him but changed her mind when she saw the two young ladies surround him again. He was smiling broadly at them and leaning his body in as he talked to them animatedly. Her eyes narrowed and she sat down again, hidden by the vase. Meanwhile Kitty was frantically texting away on her mobile and smiling broadly to herself.

Just then, all heads turned in the room when a thundering noise came from the rear end of the hall. Along with it, the wooden floorboards were vibrating.

Bette stood up at the bridal table and exclaimed to Duncan, "Oh my god, it's an earthquake!"

Suddenly, a herd of about twenty goats came jumping, leaping and trotting into the hall, bowling over a few guests as they went through. Bette stepped up onto her chair awkwardly and started to scream.

The goats were followed by a few members of the local football team, the team captain Pete pulling along their club mascot goat 'Bobby' on a lead who was outfitted with a footy jersey in their colours. Pete nodded his head apologetically to Duncan as he passed the bridal table, "Sorry mate. I got Bobby out, but the rest followed."

Some guests were laughing, but the more serious ones, they followed Bette's example and frowned at the interruption to the festivities.

"It was a surprise for you, my love," Duncan explained, pushing his glasses back on the bridge of his nose. He was helping her down from the chair, his hands firmly grasping her small waist.

But Bette glared back at him, with hands on hip, "Well, we have to get this place clean tomorrow," she snapped, her index finger pointing to mud, dirt and goat excrement trails across the floor.

"Oh bugger!" she exclaimed when she noticed her reflection in the window behind them and saw her eye makeup had run.

Raquel took her chance to be finally useful. She rushed forward, pushed her way past Kitty who was too busy texting, with her purse in hand.

"It's okay Bette. I have makeup here in case of an emergency."

"Great doll," Bette smiled at her, "You're a lifesaver. Let's go to the bathroom."

****

It had just turned twelve o'clock on a warm autumn's day.

The high school was a progressive public school and the major building was an impressive three stories high with the main original school building standing separate, positioned between the gym and the oval.

The school bell rang and echoed in the empty hallways and gradually the high school kids streamed out of the adjoining classrooms.

One of the first students out was the tall, slim and elegant Magda. In two easy strides, she arrived at her locker on the top floor, fumbled with the tiny rusty key and chucked her textbooks inside. It was a quick despatch, not a neat considerate move.

She wore her checked school dress cheekily just a centimetre above the knee and her straight dark brown hair seemed to hang down at about the same length. Her large almond shaped green eyes and long tanned legs were classic textbook schoolboy fantasy.

Her best friend Bette who was pretty, rather than a raving beauty and standing much shorter in statue, met her at the bank of lockers a few seconds later. She had a gold ribbon tied around her auburn ponytail and her school dress just touched her knees. It wasn't a cold day, but she always liked to wear her sloppy moss green school jumper over her dress. She was very self-conscious of her breasts which had grown from A cup to C cup overnight. She was also dealing with the new braces on her teeth.

"Hey," she acknowledged the arrival of her best mate.

"I was in Maths. Where were you? Your name was called out by Mr. Stewart," Bette stated in her distinctive raspy voice.

"I had a free period."

"Okay. Where's our Mandy-Jane today?"

Magda rolled her shoulders, "Don't know. Haven't seen her. Come on. Let's go behind the gym," she said in a low voice, stuffing something from her locker into her small dress pocket.

Bette dutifully followed her. After all, Magda was the self-appointed ringleader of their trio.

Safe behind the gym, with no one else around, Magda whipped out two squashed ciggies and handed one to Bette who took it, her blue eyes wide and wary. They glanced around one more time and then shared a flip lighter between them discretely.

"I shouldn't really be smoking. They reckon it stunts your growth," Bette said, holding her ciggie away at arms' length.

"Good god. For you, it's too late. How much more damage can it possibly do, shorty," remarked her much taller friend.

Magda drew back hard, and half of her cigarette was reduced to a minuscule pile of ash on the asphalt. She finally spoke again, "Shit. What a fucked day. I'd give anything to not be here, in this shithole of a bloody school."

Bette frowned but copied her example with her ciggie, which ended in a burst of her coughing, "I happen to like school, Magda, "she replied in her raspy voice, after she recovered from the coughing fit, "I'm really good at a couple of subjects, you know. And a couple of teachers seem alright."

Her friend scoffed and switched on her strange accent, "Well, good for you. But come on, get real. What are we going to do after we leave school? You're not going to be an astronaut and I'm not going to be a doctor. And Mandy-Jane, she hasn't handed in any assignments for a good month. I'm bloody sure of it."

Bette raised an eyebrow and retorted, "We can be whatever we want to be. I truly believe that."

"Fuck. Shit. Fuck," her friend squashed her ciggie into the side of a rose bush in the garden bed next to her, "Look out. Don't turn around, but Coxy's coming this way."

Bette threw her cigarette butt to the ground and stamped it out. She quickly waved the smoke away, "Crap. Did he see us?"

Mr. Cox craned his crinkled turkey neck in their direction, stopped for a moment and then he turned and headed to the music room on the other end of the building.

As he came around the corner, he nearly collided with an exuberant Mandy-Jane. She was the rough and tough one of the three friends. Her school uniforms were always three inches above her knee, her light brown hair was teased up in a punk style and she always wore a black leather choker around her neck. She also wore too much makeup. She spent half her school time in the principal's office for one thing or another, which propelled her to celebrity status among her peers. She was also eighteen years old, older than her peers. But she kept it a secret because she had been held back a couple of years at a different school.

Mandy-Jane was quite used to trouble unfortunately. Wherever her family went, trouble seemed sure to follow. Coming from a middleclass background, her family had a number of black sheep in it, rather than just the usual one. An uncle was doing jail time for breaking in and attempting to steal seven photocopiers from his former workplace. He got caught as he managed to crab step one out of the building. The second black sheep was her older brother Clive. He was often on the police radar for shoplifting and petty crime.

Mandy-Jane was not exactly an angel herself, but she was not exactly bad ass either. She grew up as a tomboy because she had four brothers to hang out with and they ran wild at the best of times. But the best kind of trouble came from next door. Being a rental property, the house hosted an impressive range of undesirable characters. There was the frisky housewife open to house calls from local tradies when her husband wasn't home. That one ended in a messy divorce, with clothes and personal belongings strewn across the front lawn. Then there was the extended Chinese family on the run from immigration, followed by the chainsaw champion who sliced and diced his way through several trees on the property. He was eventually evicted for loping the rosebushes in the front garden at six o'clock on a Sunday morning. However, the last tenants proved to be the icing on the cake and forced the landlord to sell off his investment. The 'for sale' sign went up two days after the incident happened.

Two Sundays ago, around midmorning time, Mandy-Jane had taken their family dog Barnum for a walk around the block. When she turned the corner and entered their street, she had the shock of her young life so far. The next-door neighbours were lying face down on the front lawn, with armed special task force officers positioned over them. The entire neighbourhood peered out of their front windows, watching the proceedings unfold. A drug bust was not something they saw every day. They were all to learn later that the tenants had set up a meth lab in the large back shed, which explained the strange comings and goings at all hours.

"Hello Mr. Cox," Mandy-Jane chirped cheerfully as she passed the unsmiling science teacher.

Mr. Cox cleared his throat and said in his customary, but sharp disciplinary voice,

"Keeping well? Did you do all your homework last night, Miss Fischer?"

"Yes sir."

It was a half lie, so she breezed past him before her body language gave up the gig.

Mandy-Jane trotted up to her friends, turning around briefly to see if someone was watching them, and then fished out a squashed packet of cigarettes out of her school bag to share.

"Fuck. Such an unfortunate name he has, old Coxy," she

laughed.

"Where have you been?"

"Well," she lit up a ciggie shared by Magda and swayed side to side a little too nervously, "It seems I have myself a new boyfriend. I ran a bit late this morning because of…well, you can think for yourselves. You got brains."

Bette smiled her approval, "Oh shit yeah. Who is he?"

"No. I want to keep it a secret for a while longer. Fuck. He's a great lover, you know. He's a root and a half," she said, teasingly. Mandy-Jane was the worldly one of their trio. She was the one who had experienced sex first, found out she quite liked it and was now experimenting as much as she could.

Magda pulled a face.

"Come on. Tell us? Does he go to our school? I bet he does. It's not…"

Mandy-Jane cut her off.

"No. It's a secret, guys. Can't tell you, but tonight, like, it's going to be magic. We are taking it to another level. I guess I can tell you this much. He says he really loves me. He tells me he wants to tie me up and do…all this sex stuff to me. Erotic type stuff, you know what I mean. Like, wow."

Bette looked at her with a mix of shock and admiration on her face, "That's sounds scary. Crazy scary."

"Bloody sexy but crazy scary," Magda added, "I wouldn't trust someone to do that to me. I hope you know what you're doing, MJ. 'Cos if he ties you up, he could be doing anything to you."

"Magda, I think I can trust him," Mandy-Jane was immediately on the defensive and flicked her eyes to the sky, "Hey, he's my boyfriend. And he loves me. I do things for him, like he says no one else can. He says I'm his special girl."

Her two friends stared silently at each other, sharing the same thoughts but said nothing in return to her. The trio of school friends had another five minutes together before the school bell rang out. They returned to their respective classes.

The next time they got together, it was after school had finished that day.

Magda and Bette waited impatiently at the bank of lockers for Mandy-Jane to appear. They waited for ten minutes before giving up and heading towards the school front gates, their heavy school bags slung over their shoulders.

"Don't know where she got to," Bette shook her head, her auburn ponytail swinging behind her.

Magda bit her lip, "She's hooked on that boyfriend, whoever he is. He's splitting our little group up."

"I can't imagine not being around you guys, ever."

Magda stopped in her tracks very suddenly, forcing Bette to sidestep, "There she is."

Bette narrowed her eyes and shielded them with a cupped hand from the sun's intense glare. All she could see was a girl's bottom as she was leaning through the drivers' side window of a white car parked out in the street. She realised the school dress was just short enough to belong to Mandy Jane.

"Hey MJ," Magda yelled out, "Are you coming?"

Their friend turned around and smiled in acknowledgment. They could not see who she was talking to. They were obscured by her cute figure half leaning in the car window. She flicked her light brown hair playfully and turned back to continue the conversation with the driver.

"Must be the new boyfriend," Bette whispered.

"You're probably right. Can't believe she's too busy to

bloody talk to us."

She shrugged her shoulders, "So? She really likes him. It's not a crime, is it."

They saw Mandy-Jane turn around one more time, grinning and waving at them. Her besties waved back and kept on walking out of the school gates. They left her to talk to the stranger sitting in the car.

That was the last time they ever saw her, as Mandy-Jane Fischer mysteriously disappeared later that day. She never made it home to her family. Her disappearance was dismissed at first. She had been known to be a bit of a rebel. Sometimes she was away for a couple of days but always returned.

After two days passed with no word, the search was seriously on. Her smiling face flashed up on news reports and stared out from the front pages of the newspapers.

Her body was found eight days later. She was discovered floating face down in the local reservoir. Four suspects were uncovered, but no one was ever convicted of the crime. The students in her year eventually left school and moved to the next stage of their lives. As time passed by, Mandy-Jane's mysterious death became a distant memory to them and the general public.

Chapter Three

Word of someone swimming in the local dam reached the charismatic Phil Proctor who was engaged in an intimate conversation with a farmers' young wife in the hall. He was whispering sweet somethings in her ear when he heard the commotion happening around them.

Someone had shouted out, "Hey. There's someone swimming in the dam."

Proctor turned his head and frowned, "Hell. Why would somebody swim…unless they're trapped."

Proctor immediately got up, took off his Stetson hat and rolled up the sleeves of his blue denim shirt.

"My apologies to you, ma'am," he said to the young woman who looked put out by the turn of events, then he turned to a broad red headed guy who looked ready to take action himself, he told him, "I got a tow rope in my truck. I'll just go get it for us to use."

Proctor raced to his vehicle and then jogged down to the dam, like a man half his age.

By the time the rope was thrown down and Phil Proctor and the young farmer managed to reach the waters' edge, Kitty was barely alive. Her head had slipped under the murky dark water for a long minute. Fortunately for her, Proctor had slipped down the muddy embankment and had plunged into the dam up to his shoulder blades. Using his strong tanned muscular arms, he very quickly scooped her up in them. When they finally dragged her exhausted body up the embankment, Kitty was covered in mud from head to toe so no one even knew who she was. Her long hair was plastered against her body. She could no longer make a sound and she was slipping in and out of consciousness.

Proctor immediately took command of the situation and he shouted out instructions. He wrapped a clean blanket which had magically appeared around her cold, muddy body and tried to keep her awake but she did not respond. By the time the paramedics arrived thirty minutes later, she was close to death. She went into cardiac arrest but was quickly revived by the paramedics. In the meantime, Proctor had walked away and washed his muddied hands in the toilets. He also grabbed a large towel to wrap around his dirty shirt and muddy jeans. The paramedics had cleaned her face with a few wet wipes and when he returned, Proctor finally recognised her.

"Oh, goddamn it," he cursed under his breath. He took his shirt off and wiped his freshly soiled hands on a clean hand towel thrown to him by a farmer.

He stood there in shock, brushing a hand through his silver-grey hair as Duncan's new wife came running up. She dropped her tiers of ruffles at a safe, clean distance and totally puffed, she said, "What happened? Someone in the hall has been saying someone's dead. I hope it's not true."

"It's your bridesmaid. Yes, ma'am. Your old' pal from Sydney. We just pulled her out of the dam."

"Kitty," she yelled out and tried to rush forward, but Proctor waved her back.

"It's okay. It's okay. They will take good care of her, Missy. She can't hear you."

As they placed Kitty gently on the gurney and pushed her towards the ambulance, she looked like a skinny girl sleeping deeply. The ambulance van doors shut soundly behind her.

Tears streamed down Bette's cheeks and disappeared into her heaving cleavage as she watched her good friend leave in the ambulance. Bette buried her head against Proctor's chest. Duncan made his appearance and looked accusingly at Proctor who was standing next to his new wife, now stripped down to his waist with the towel tucked around his damp jeans. To his credit, Proctor had his strong, still muddy arms raised away from touching Bette or her wedding dress.

"What the hell's going on here?"

"Look. Your wife's model pal, she fell into the dam, and we fished her out. She's in a bad way I reckon. Your poor wife's just upset at the moment. That's why, she's a bit too close."

Duncan's bright blue eyes widened behind his glasses and his tone softened, "Shit. Okay. That's fine. Hug her."

Bette lifted her head away from Proctor's warm, heaving chest and through her tears she said, "But I want you to hug me."

"You know what this means, don't you?" Duncan sighed.

Bette sniffed and rubbed her eyes. Her eye makeup was now smeared all over her face, "No, what are you on about, Phil?"

"I might be called in, to investigate what happened here tonight."

"You can't do that…we're off to Bali tomorrow evening."

"Just saying. Now come on. Let's go back to the party and

we can check up on her later. Come on, honey."

Bette pulled away from Proctor and patted her tear-stained cheeks.

She said, "I have to clean myself up in the ladies."

Proctor looked down at himself and grinned broadly, "I might have to get myself into a goddamn shower. I'll re-join your great soiree later. Was enjoying myself immensely. It's a great shindig."

****

Bette Duncan giggled merrily as her husband carried her, her massive wedding dress with all its layers of ruffles and a glass of French champagne in hand over the threshold of their marital bedroom.

He settled her gently onto the bed and she immediately struck a sexy, come hither pose for him. She roughly placed her champagne glass on the bedside table. He rested his glasses neatly on the nearby blanket box, removed his tie with a sweeping gesture and bent over her.

"Didn't you love today?"

She smiled ever so slightly, "Yes, except the bloody goats and then, my poor darling Kitty. I hope she's going to be alright. Poor dear girl."

Duncan sighed, "The goats were a bit of fun. But the other matter. That was unfortunate. They might ask me to investigate, you know, my love."

His wife flicked her hair and made her thoughts on that subject clear to him,

"Well, you won't be doing that, getting involved. It's too close to home. They can't really expect to involve you.

Another detective can do as well."

"Well now, Mrs. Duncan," his voice was a seductive half growl, "We are finally alone. Left to our own devices, so to speak."

"Yes, we are. Take it all off," she teased him, pulling down one shoulder strap of her dress.

"Hey you. Come here, my lovely, darling wife," he held her shoulders and kissed her eager, hungry lips long and hard. He lay down on top of her and started gently nuzzling her pale soft throat.

"Do you want to play a game of 'you're under arrest'?" he murmured, opening a bedside drawer to reveal a set of shiny Police issue handcuffs.

"Not tonight, dear. It's a bit heavy handed for one's wedding night," she sighed, running a teasing forefinger along his strong jawline.

"Okay. Well, what about 'you're needed down at the station for a witness statement'," he opened the second bedside drawer to reveal a notepad and a tube of strawberry scented lubricant.

"No."

At this point, he realised he had to pour on the charm. His right hand started searching for his prize waiting under the multitude of layers and folds of her wedding dress. She started to moan in his ear when his fingers found her wet pussy and lingered there. But his attention to detail was unfortunately distracted by his mobile phone ringing in his trouser back pocket.

"Damn it. Ignore it. Turn it off. Get rid of it," she whispered, her eyes half shut.

"Sorry my love," he gently kissed her forehead but did not

immediately withdraw his hand.

He repositioned himself onto the bed, put his glasses back on and felt for his mobile with his left hand.

"I can't dismiss it. Could be work calling me."

She rolled her eyes, "Bloody hell, tell 'em you're far too busy pleasuring your wife. We've started our honeymoon."

"Can't say that," he took a deep breath and answered, "Hello, this is Senior Detective Phillip Duncan."

Bette lay back perfectly still as Duncan sat there, listening for a long minute.

"Okay. I understand but I am officially on my honeymoon. If you weren't aware of it, I was married today…yes, well, thank you."

He winked playfully at her. She stared back, looking unimpressed. But his fingers were still caressing her clitoris and she relaxed again, breathing deeply.

Another long minute passed, before he could say a few more words. Then unfortunately for her, he withdrew his hand from under the folds of her dress.

"Not an accident? Okay. Well, I can go to the hospital in the morning."

Bette shook her head at him and mouthed the word 'no'. But Duncan raised his forefinger to his lips and kept on talking. He also pushed his glasses back on the bridge of his nose.

"I will look into it… No, I wasn't exactly there when she was rescued."

Another long pause.

"Okay, will check it out. I'll talk to you tomorrow…Yeah. Bye…Yes, thank you. Nice of you to say."

Bette Duncan sat up and looked at her husband critically,

"Oh please. Don't tell me. You are going to investigate what happened tonight at the dam. Just because you happen to live in Brumby Flat now, they can't expect you to drop everything. We just got married. For god's sake."

"Sorry. Got to investigate what went on tonight," he said in his quiet voice, hoping it would calm her down.

"Right now, I care about us. This is supposed to be the start of our new life together, Phillip."

"I know my love. But you have to understand. I have been in my job for a long, long time. It's important work that I do."

She folded her arms and sat upright, "Today was our day. Tonight, should be for us. Nothing else in the world should matter."

Detective Phillip Duncan got up off their martial bed and peered down through his glasses at his new wife. He visibly frowned at her. What he had told her might happen, had now come true.

"How can you say that? Bette, I have been asked to investigate an attempted murder. It may have been an accident, you know. Maybe she just fell into the dam, but I need to find out what the truth is. And she's your old friend too. Where's your compassion for Kitty?"

"Well, yes. Drowning in a dam, accidents can happen. It's not like it doesn't happen, Phil. She probably slipped on some mud and she bloody fell in. And that's that. There's probably no need to investigate. Let them call someone else in to look into it."

"I have to find that out, my love. It's what I do."

Bette's eyes started to well up with tears and then she leaned forward and grabbed his left arm in a desperate gesture, "Look. We just got married, and the plane leaves for

Bali tomorrow night. Please. Don't let me go on my own, and I promise you, I will. I will go to Bali without you, Phillip."

Her grip on his arm was tight, but he wrestled out of it easily enough and stepped back, out of her reach.

"What is wrong with you?" he said in a low, stern voice, "I have a job to do. And it's very important to me. She's your best friend, Kitty Caulfield who was at your wedding. Now, she's lying in a coma in the hospital and you're being so bloody selfish."

She started to cry hysterically, "At our wedding, our wedding, Phil."

He clicked his tongue the way he usually did. His nerves were rattled, and he was trying hard to think straight.

"Okay, Mrs. Bette Duncan. I don't know what the hell's wrong with you. I think I'll sleep in one of the other rooms tonight. We'll talk things over later. Well. Anyway. Good night my love," he turned and opened the door to leave. She looked at him with pleading big blue eyes, but he chose to ignore them.

Once outside their bedroom, he leaned back against the closed door, undoing his white shirt cuffs and cufflinks in annoyance.

Under his breath, he muttered, "Brumby bloody Flat strikes again."

He could clearly hear his new wife sobbing behind the bedroom door. He wanted to go back in. He wanted to apologise and sweep her up into his arms, beg her forgiveness but he couldn't allow himself to do it. He had sworn an oath and allegiance to the police force and to uphold the law.

He heaved a long, heavy sigh. He was about to take the stairs up to one of the spare B&B rooms, when a staggering, fairly drunk Phil Proctor appeared around the corner. He had a long tanned sinewy arm curled over a local farmer's wife. She was a little plump around the hips and upper arms, but had a wide pretty face, framed by shoulder length ash brown curls. She was giggling and fluttering her big brown eyes up at Proctor. There was no doubt there was a sexual chemistry around the pair. There was no doubt in Duncan's mind what they had planned to do about it too.

Proctor grinned back at the detective, even dipping his hat to him. He had managed to get cleaned up after the dip in the dam and had changed into clean clothes he had stashed in the back of his pickup truck. He had swapped his hats around too. He pressed his finger against his lips and said, "Hey, Mate, Congratulations again. Now, what goes on under the roof of this great establishment, stays quiet, don't it?"

Duncan shook his head, "Look. If she asks me, I won't tell a lie. I knew her before you made an appearance in town."

Proctor and the farmer's wife stood there looking at him, swaying slightly in unison. Then Proctor hugged his new companions' arm and admired her beaming face in the half light, "Oh well, my sweet. Are you still interested in sharing a secret, just between the two of us?"

"Of course," she chirped, "I like you, cowboy. Dead set, I'm mad keen on you."

"Whoa, not too keen my darling girl. It's a bit complicated for me. I am not into sentimental bull shit."

"You said it. The room left of the stairs is free. By the way, Proctor. Don't leave town," Duncan snapped as he quickly bolted up the stairs to find a spare bedroom himself and crash for the night.

****

Raquel heard the front door of Proctor's cottage creak on its hinges. She had been waiting in the lounge room for much of the morning, curled up on the couch, ready to strike like a brown snake disturbed.

"Hey, Phil. You're back, I see. You didn't come home last night. Do you know what time it is?" Raquel snapped at him, as he tried to walk quietly through the hallway. He had a hand up to his throbbing right temple, dealing with a slight hangover as well as the shrill snap of her accusing voice which followed him. Maxine their cattle dog who had been also curled up on the couch next to her, lowered her ears and not a fan of her masters' raised voices, she slipped away to lie low in the adjacent dining room.

Proctor turned to Raquel and inclined his head, as if the burden of guilt was genuinely weighing him down. He looked at her for a moment but said nothing in his defence. He strode quietly into the kitchen, with Raquel still shadowing him.

"I saw you, Tex. I saw *who* you left the hall with the other night. It was that Hayseed woman. She's married by the way, but I suppose you don't care."

Proctor coughed and said, "Her name's Mrs. Haywood. And what the Hell's matter with you anyway, why you're calling me 'Tex' all of a sudden?"

"Seed, wood, same thing. I am surprised at your behaviour last night. But carrying on with a married woman. A local farmer's wife? Wow. That's such a stupid, stupid thing to do in a small town like this. How could you do this to me? I really thought…"

He turned on his heel and finished her sentence with a flourish, "I loved you? Yeah Missy. I do. I love you, my sweetheart, but you are not easy to love these days. I feel you don't seriously understand me anymore, ma'am. For a while now, you have been shutting me down and shutting me out."

Raquel said nothing, her arms folded in front of her chest.

"Well, at any rate I have finished my silo work. I'm not taking on another project here. And my father is coming out of Texas to see me and then we're going back to the states together. It's time for me to move on, my girlie. It's been real fun, for sure."

Raquel turned around and studied him closely, "What? Your father's actually still alive? How old would he be then?"

"Yes ma'am. And he's a proud Texan statesman through and through. Everything's bigger and better in Texas, you know. He'll tell you that, no fear. Every day he'll be telling you that, ma'am. I guess I'd better go…"

He had turned to look at her, but she had already walked out of the back door of the kitchen. She didn't want him to see her tears and how upset she really was. She was certain he had screwed the Haywood farmer's wife.

She ran into the stables, sobbing. She stopped there to stroke the long, sleek forehead of the black mare. She was trying to pull herself together, but the tears continued to flow. She was sick and tired of Proctor's carefree attitude and disregard for her feelings. It was hard to take because they had seemed to be so close, so perfect for each other.

She didn't want to move back into her house next to the Raindrops Shop. But she also realised that it was not a good idea to continue to exist under the same roof with someone who had no genuine regard for her feelings. She wiped her tears away and realised she had a significant, tough decision to make.

Chapter Four

The day after the night before, Steve Willaston was asked by his immediate superior to speak to a couple of local key eyewitnesses who were standing near the dam on the night of Bette and Phil's wedding reception. When he had finished taking down their statements and personal observations, he drove towards Proctor's cottage on the hill, hoping to say hello to his mother. But he was distracted driving through the township when he saw all the signs out for the local country market. He had lived in Brumby Flat on and off for over two years, and had never once been to its' country market.

Strangely, he was drawn to stop and look it over that day. It appeared to be very popular as he had to park the police car halfway down the main road. People, locals and strangers were streaming into the reserve from every direction.

He nodded and smiled at a couple of locals he knew managing their stalls of goods and produce. He proceeded to walk down the first aisle. He was impressed by the variety of stalls, which included jewellery, plants, wind chimes, wooden toys and Bric-a-brac.

Then he saw her. She was looking after the last stall on the very end of the aisle. The sight of her knocked the breath out of him almost instantly. Kristina 'Yankee' Tanaka stood nearly as tall as he did. She was standing aloof behind a table full of miniature Viking and dragon boats, bonsai's, small delicate Japanese bowls and a large platter of freshly made sushi rolls. She flicked her very long, smooth brown hair over one shoulder and he was able to admire her large almond eyes, perfectly balanced by a wide flat nose and full lips. Her face was a perfect white porcelain. She wore a simple cropped white T-shirt with a well-worn, faded pair of old hipster jeans flared down from the knee. He could see her pale taunt midriff. Her facial features, straight hair and willowy frame suggested her oriental ancestry, however she clearly had half her looks from somewhere else. Or at least, at this moment of time, he couldn't work out the where from, but her mixed features were unusually attractive to him.

Steve held his breath, sucked in his stomach, straightened his police uniform and summoned up the courage to go over to her stall. He would have to strike up a conversation with her.

He expected her to notice him in his smart uniform, but she did not even raise her eyes from her mobile phone. She had started texting someone somewhere else.

"Hi, nice day," he said very brightly.

She just nodded and keep texting away with both thumbs.

"Well, what have you got here?"

She signed heavily and kept on texting away, "You have eyes, you can see."

He noted she had a slight American accent to her speech.

"So many nice things here. Can you help pick something out for my mother? It's her birthday coming up," he lied. "Can you suggest something I can get for her?"

"Yeah, I suggest you look for something you know she likes. I don't know your mother personally."

"Yes, it's probably true."

She stopped texting and glared at him, her almond eyes burning bright, "Hey. If you don't have the money, Mr. Policeman, don't bother me. I am, like, here to sell, not to talk small talk type stuff."

"Did you make all of this?" he asked her after a minute of uncomfortable silence.

"Gawd, it's not me. My parents make all this stuff up, All handmade. I'm just minding the stall for them. They should be back any minute."

"They're very talented."

She rolled her eyes and inclined her head to the left, "Yeah well, you can tell them in person what you think."

Her parents appeared. Her father smiled at him and immediately thrust his hand forward. Steve shook it very firmly, "Hello, I'm Mr. Tanaka. This is my wife Leena," he said with a strong American accent. "You have met our Yankee, I see."

His wife flashed him an icy cold look under her light brown perfect fringe, so he very quickly corrected the situation, "I mean, our lovely Kristina. Are we in any trouble, Officer?"

Steve smirked, "Oh no sir, just getting some fresh air and looking around the market. You have nice stuff here."

Mr. Tanaka grinned, while his pale, blue eyed wife looked him up and down in a quiet, reserved way.

Steve now understood where Kristina's exotic look came from. Her father was tall and clearly Asian and her mother had an Eastern European background. Steve was to find out

She then turned the book pages upside down, "Well, this position looks very difficult. Requires some elevation, I think. I'll have to go first, and then you follow me."

"Okay Mrs. Tanaka, let's go."

Two years later, after they had settled into their first home in Kansas, they welcomed their first daughter Kristina. Three years later, along came Celine who was conceived around the time of their return trip to Las Vegas to celebrate the fifth anniversary of their wedding.

Good but strict parents, they made sure the girls always made it to their folk dancing classes, baseball practise, piano lessons, jazz ballet and Jiu-jitsu classes. To motive the girls, Mr. Tanaka used to say to them 'without culture, we are oarless in the water.' He stopped saying it after young Celine kept asking him innocently "where is the water?" He changed it to 'Our culture is central to everything we do and feel.' The girls did not question that one.

After some consideration for what was best for their children's future, the Tanaka's' decided to make the big move to Australia. Leena wanted to live in fast paced Sydney but Mr. Tanaka preferred cosmopolitan Melbourne.

In the end, they wanted to ensure they had plenty of savings left over, so they settled for the small town of Brumby Flat in South Australia instead. They were able to buy a large new home for cheap and also, they were told the country markets were very popular and possibly their best source of future income. They made the move two years ago and bought a five-bedroom home with an enormous family room at the rear. They converted one bedroom into a craft room and another larger space into a dance studio for their folk dancing. The girls were both very good students and were accepted immediately by their new school and their peers.

Leena stood there at the country market with folded arms, staring down Constable Steve Willaston. Finally, she said quietly, "I am happy you like our work."

Mr. Tanaka looked surprised at his wife, as he raised an eyebrow, "Well, we spend time on what we do. You live here, in town too?"

Steve nodded, twirling his police hat in his hands, "Yeah, in, out and around. Anyway, I keep an eye on things. I'm Constable Steve Willaston. I don't reckon I introduced myself before."

Leena pushed up the corners of her lips a little, which was her attempt at a smile, "Well, Constable. You must come and visit our humble home one day. We live behind that church down the road."

"Thanks. I'd love that."

"Mr. Steve, help yourself to a couple of sushi rolls. Take some with you, free. I make them real good, real fresh," Mr. Tanaka said, waving his hand excitedly over the platter.

"Ah. I'd better not Sir, but thank you. I'd better get going. I'm in the middle of this big investigation. Nice to meet you guys. Hey, see you around Kristina."

He nodded in their beautiful daughters' direction and she very briefly fluttered her almond gold flecked eyes at him and brushed her long brown hair out with her willowy fingers. Then she returned to her frantic texting. She was aloof, exactly like her mother. But Steve Willaston was hopelessly and completely infatuated with her. He looked back a couple of times as he walked away.

****

It was around seven o'clock in the evening. It had been another scorching hot summers' day but it was beginning to cool down. The people of Brumby Flat were starting to slowly creep outdoors, walking their dogs, walking just themselves or pruning plants and bushes in their front gardens. It was the perfect way for all the locals to watch or find out from their neighbours what was happening in town.

A police car quietly pulled up to a stop in a side street. It seemed the whole of Brumby Flat stared as a familiar figure emerged from the driver's seat.

Constable Steve Willaston on his local beat, held his breath and then knocked on the front door of 'Yankee' Tanaka's family home. It was a newly built home, rendered white with a vivid blue tin roof. He was still on official duty, looking neat and proud in his dark navy police uniform. He rolled on his heels until the front door swung open.

Yankee's father stood in the hallway, eyes blinking hard against the last glimmer of sunlight.

"Oh, hello Mr. Steve," he said in his clipped English with a strong American lilt, "You here on business? What's wrong? Am I about to be arrested?"

He gave Steve a little wink and chuckled.

Steve smiled, "Oh no, sir. Just come for a short visit. Your wife invited me to visit your home, last weekend. If you remember."

Mr Tanaka winked and raised a forefinger, "Ah yes, you come to see my Yankee girl. Come in, come in. Oh, you have to leave shoes outside."

Mr. Tanaka pointed to the neat row of shoes lined up on the left side of their front veranda.

"I'm sorry sir, but I can't," Steve bowed a little, "I am still on duty, you see."

"Oh. Alright. Come in but you walk on tip toe. My Mrs. Tanaka is very..well, she's a clean freak. She won't like it."

Steve dutifully followed him through the long hallway with its shiny Baltic pine floor, into their sunken bright red loungeroom filled with ornaments. Miniatures of Viking boats and dragon boats vied for attention on the mantelpiece amidst a cluster of his Estonian wife's collection of colourful folk costumed dolls which stared down the elegant Japanese geisha-like porcelain figurines book ending them.

There was an odd mix of oriental styled furniture and a selection of Scandinavian oak style furniture jostling for space.

His eyes locked instantly on Kristina Tanaka who was casually curled up on their enormous white modular lounge, watching the television which seemed to dominate the room. She looked so beautiful and serene, the sight of her took his breath away as usual. Her long dark hair framed her face and her fringe sat perfectly straight above her large almond eyes which complemented her bee sting lips, inherited from her Estonian mother. She wore a plain white singlet and black fleece trackie pants, but she made it look like haute couture on her. She had rolled up the track pants to her knees, showing off her long, willowy pale legs which were crossed together casually on the lounge. Seated beside her, her much younger sister was playing with her hair with one hand and picking at a bowl of popcorn with her other. She looked like a younger version of her sister, blessed with the same striking features. Her little sister noticed Steve first and Kristina glanced at him quickly then averted her eyes back to the television.

"Yankee honey, here is your good friend, Mister local

policeman," her father announced.

"Constable Steve Willaston," he added with too much enthusiasm.

"He's not my friend. He's not anything, Dad," she replied coolly.

"Be nice. Remember your manners please, Kristina."

"It's okay Mr. Tanaka. I won't arrest her for saying that."

"Sit down. Please. Relax."

"Well, okay. I am still on duty."

Steve squeezed his way into the lounge between Kristina and her sister Celine. Kristina visibly rolled her eyes and flicked her long brown hair in obvious annoyance.

Her father noticed and spoke rapidly in Japanese to her. She replied sharply in Estonian.

"You want a drink?" he asked Steve politely.

"No. Thanks for asking. I'm actually a bit hungry."

Kristina grunted and without as much as a sideward glance, she shoved a bowl of popcorn directly under his nose.

"Yeah, uh, thanks for that."

"Yankee. Tell the nice policeman here about your ambition."

When she remained quiet, he continued himself enthusiastically, "She just finished high school this year. Finished top of her class in all subjects."

Steve grinned, "That's great. Are you planning to go to Uni?" he asked her.

She flicked her eyes up for a second, "No. I have applied to this big new Space agency. I believe I would do well strapped to one of their gravity-defying machines. I have nerves of steel."

"Yeah? I don't doubt it."

Her proud father sat down in his favourite armchair with carved dragon legs and plush red velvet upholstery. He started to laugh, slapping his right knee hard.

"Hey, do you wanna hear a good story, Steve?"

Steve rolled his shoulders, "Sure. Okay."

"You know why I call this one Yankee?" he said, winking at him and baiting his eldest daughter.

"Dad, please, not this story again," she snapped, folding her arms.

"Yes, but it is good story. Wait a minute, wait a minute. In Kansas, before she was born, her mother and me, we are watching television on couch. It's big match, but not the final Superbowl match. My team is The Yankees. They are playing. Mother's team is Vikings but they are not playing then. Her mother very heavy, she looks ready to burst. She's sitting on the couch next to me. My Yankees are going for a really big home run and my wife, she turns to me, says I feel funny. I say not now, home run is coming. My wife yells at me, the baby is coming she says to me. Very, very loud in my ear. I am now deaf."

At this point, Mr. Tanaka got up and demonstrated with an enthused series of actions, "My wife, she stands up and baby just about here. Boom. Bam. She's suddenly here. It's my little Yankee. I have home run in my home, as well as on the TV. My Yankees win and I call her Yankee. But wife says no, Kristina is a much better name. But she's always my little 'Yankee' Tanaka."

He ended his story with a cheeky wink.

His eldest daughter said some choice words in a mix of Estonian and Japanese and sunk down as far as she could go into their lounge suite.

"Oh my god, Dad. You're so embarrassing."

"But it's a true story. You know. I love my little Yankee from the minute she shoot out into the world."

Steve smirked, trying not to laugh out loud. He just nodded.

Finally, he said, "That's a lovely story, Mr. Tanaka. Wow. What an entrance."

"Yeah. She's been like that forever. She always makes entrance. I should know. Now, this young one over here…"

He wagged his forefinger at younger sister Celine who giggled shyly. She hid her pretty oval face with those same bee sting lips in her cupped hands.

"Her mother and I went to Vegas. We saw Celine, she's a very good singer, you know. What a voice. Then baby two is born in hospital. For a change, something different. This baby, well, mate. She screams in this really big voice. I say to my wife, it's my turn now. I name this little one. She is Celine Tanaka for sure."

Steve chuckled openly this time, because Kristina looked smug now that the attention had been drawn to her shy little sister.

"Where is your wife?"

Mr. Tanaka smiled, "My Leena is at the local market in the next town today, selling her dolls and Baltic craft. She is amazing woman. So smart, she's sharp and we are really, what they say, we are soulmates. Okay?"

He turned to watch the television. With his attention now diverted, Kristina leaned her bare shoulder against Steve's arm, and she whispered only low enough for him to hear what she said.

"If you cuff me, you've got me."

He shivered at her light touch on his arm and stared back at her in astonishment, her long straight hair brushed across his wrist and he could smell the apple scented shampoo that she used. He felt certain that he was blushing.

"Well, okay. I had no plans, but I guess I'd better work on it now." He whispered back.

She nodded her pretty head, flicked her long brown hair back and took out her mobile phone to send off some text messages. She had stated her interest. That was enough for now.

Suddenly, they heard the back door unlock and the screen door slide open quite dramatically. Leena Tanaka appeared; her demeanour cool but slightly ruffled. She was wearing an elegant no nonsense maroon pant suit with a long strand of amber beads against her chest. Her light brown hair was flicked up at the tips against her slender neck.

"Honey, my love," Mr. Tanaka smiled and raised his right hand, "You're home early. Look, we have a visitor."

Leena gave Steve a quick, stern glance and then averted her cool blue eyes back to her husband, "I saw the police car outside. I thought something awful had happened."

"No. All good here. How was your market?"

"It was a complete waste of time. Sold two boats only. One dragon, one Viking. Just covered the market stall fee. Not going back to that one."

Standing with hands on hip, she took a longer look at Steve and then started talking rapidly in Estonian and Mr. Tanaka replied back, a bit slower and carefully considering his words.

A few moments later, they were exchanging words in Japanese. Very loudly.

Finally, they returned to English.

Leena slowly sat down in one of their generous Scandi armchairs with a hand embroidered cushion on it and said in a quiet, low voice, "I am sorry. It is very rude of us to speak a different language in front of visitors, but I notice you are wearing your shoes inside our home."

"I am still on duty. My apologies Mrs. Tanaka."

"My carpet is pristine, white and fluffy. And that's exactly how I like it to be."

Steve nodded in understanding and got up to leave.

Leena sighed, and stretched her hand out to him, "It's alright. Please, sit, sit. But if there's any dirt left behind on my good carpet, I expect you'll clean it up."

"Of course, Mrs. Tanaka."

By now, Mr. Tanaka could sense his wife's prickly mood.

"I have to go and unpack the car," Leena said sternly.

Her husband waved his hand in the air and quickly replied, "It's okay. I will do it, my darling dear. Back soon, kids."

Steve stayed for another fifteen minutes but he noticed the room dynamics had changed with the arrival of Leena Tanaka. He said his goodbyes and crept out carefully on the tips of his shoes.

Chapter Five

"What? You're joking? Fuckin' seriously? She's gone flying off to the Bali honeymoon without you?" Detective Longmeil exclaimed, putting on his best long face and leaning forward, his elbows on the massive granite benchtop in Bette and Duncan's kitchen.

"Unbelievable. That must feel pretty raw for you."

Duncan nodded, pressing his glasses back onto the bridge of his nose, "I know. I didn't expect her to really do it."

"How do you know she's done that?"

Duncan sighed heavily, "Aside from the fact that I'm a Detective by profession, I could see the booklet of Bali tickets had gone from our bedside table. And her suitcase too. It wasn't too hard to work it all out."

Duncan secretly wished he had not told Detective Longmeil what was happening with his marriage. But it was too late. He had already vented and taken his work partner into his confidence. His private life was unfortunately now in the open. Longmeil had a reputation for passing on gossip in the office.

Duncan got up on cue and took the whistling kettle off the stove top and started to prepare their coffees. He splashed the milk accidentally into Longmeil's mug. Just a bit too much.

His work partner shook his head, "Maybe you should've taken leave when you married her, Phil."

"Well, unfortunately I didn't foresee an attempted murder in Brumby bloody Flat at my own wedding, did I? Anyway, the department has been quiet."

"So, what are you going to do? About your wife, I mean."

Duncan rolled his shoulders and took another sip of instant coffee in his kitchen at Bette's home. At this moment of time, he didn't feel like it was their shared home.

"I can't do much really. If I call her, she'll probably get all upset at me. I'll just let her enjoy her honeymoon her way. Alone. When my Bette gets back, we'll have a good, long talk about it. Hopefully we can work things out."

Longmeil then changed the subject, much to Duncan's relief, "I guess there's no change at the hospital with Caulfield."

Duncan shook his head, "No. She's still in a coma. I'll check in on her again tomorrow."

Meanwhile, on the other side of town, Raquel was busy opening up the Raindrops Shop for the day. She had promised Bette that she would still open for a couple of days. She wasn't used to early mornings anymore, so her hair was unbrushed but at least, she was dressed smartly in a white shirt teamed with an orange pleated skirt. As she struggled with the key and finally unlocked the shop door, her mobile phone rang.

"Hello?"

She recognised her good friends raspy voice, "It's just me, doll. I'm over here, in Bali."

"Oh wow. I wasn't expecting to hear from you. I mean, you're on your honeymoon."

"I'm here in Bali on my own," she added.

"What? Where's Phil? What's happened?"

Raquel put the phone down on the shop countertop with loudspeaker on as she opened the till and started to count the float money.

"Home. He's investigating you know where and you know what."

"Oh no. You're kidding me. So, you left him? Have you left him?"

There was a short silence on the phone before Bette finally said, "Perhaps, I have. I don't know. I'm not happy that he put his work before me. I know it's terrible about poor Kitty being in hospital. Anyway, I have put it all behind me and I am enjoying myself at the resort. It's just beautiful in Bali. They have everything here and I've found someone else to enjoy my time with."

Raquel nearly dropped the coffee cup she was carrying to the coffee machine.

"Bette, you just got married three days ago. You said to me you love Phillip Duncan. Bloody hell. You told me he was the love of your life. You even got the tattoo to prove it. You can't just go away on your honeymoon on your own and find a new guy!" She exclaimed.

"I really didn't plan to meet anyone, doll. It just happened. He's a real gentleman from New Zealand. Looking after me very well, and I'm about to join him for a cocktail by the pool. Please. Don't say anything to my Phil. It's probably just a holiday fling thing but I did tell the guy what my current situation is."

Raquel wiped a stray tear from the corner of her eye. For reasons she couldn't fathom, she felt sorry for Detective

Duncan.

"But Bette, that's not right. Your current situation is you're a married woman now. Don't you think you've overreacted just a little bit? I mean, your husband is trying to find out what happened to your best friend."

"No way, doll," "she retorted angrily, raising her voice, "You don't understand. You don't know the full story. He should've put me first. He should've put our marriage first. Someone else could be doing this investigation but he accepted it, in front of me, on our wedding night."

"Well…I am sure Phil is miserable without you."

"He's okay. He's so bloody immersed in his work to know anything else. How's my shop going anyway?"

"I've just opened. No customers yet. A bit early still. Please Bette, don't worry about the shop. I promised you I'd look after things for you."

She heard Bette's mood finally lifted on the other end of the phone, "I know you will, doll. I trust you. My love to you and Kitty. Talk again soon."

The mobile call ended and she placed it back on the countertop.

Raquel stood still for a moment, trying to comprehend what was happening. But she didn't have too much time to herself to process everything when a familiar face entered the shop. It was a shock for her at first.

Anabella Williams smiled back, showing off her fire engine red lippy. Her silvery grey hair was teased into a massive beehive, and she was wearing a groovy pair of cat's eyes sunnies. Instead of her usual flirty and frilly nineteen-fifties dresses, her perfectly slim frame barely filled out a bright floral orange shift. Teamed with bright yellow tights and a pair of pointed black ankle boots, she looked like she had walked straight out of a nineteen-sixties' film set.

"Hey Anabella!" "Raquel exclaimed, "My god, it's you. I had no idea you were back in town. Great to see you again."

"Lovely to see you too. I got out over a week ago. It's taken me a little bit of time to get out of the house," she was struggling to express her feelings, "This is a big change for me. Being outside, I mean. But…here I am. You didn't visit me ever."

Raquel took a deep intake of breath and said, "Yes, I'm sorry. It's been a busy couple of years. Life got in the way, that's all that happened. No other reason, believe me."

Anabella smiled and brought forward the tray of cupcakes she had been hiding behind her back, "Never mind. I brought these in for you. Baked them fresh this morning," she proclaimed proudly.

"Oh wow. Thank you, for *me*?"

"Oh yes. It's for you, Bette and the shop. They're my pineapple upside down cupcakes. I haven't been able to cook for ages, so I hope they turned out okay."

Raquel hesitated for a moment, remembering why Anabella had gone to jail in the first place, then took a quick whiff over the tray, "Wow, they smell great. How about I make us a coffee and let's share one of these babies together."

She nodded, "Alright."

She sat down at one of the narrow coffee tables, crossing her slim, long legs under her knees. She removed her sunglasses and placed them carefully on top of her forehead. Raquel busied herself with the secret workings of the coffee machine. She wasn't a very good barista, but she persisted at it.

"How's the shop been going?"

Raquel looked over the splattering coffee machine and replied, "It's quieter than it used to be. The tourist trade has dropped off a bit. The murder town tag has finally left us too. The café is the busy part of the business these days."

Anabella nodded her head, "Well, that's good. It was an awful time. We were all scared, worried if we were going to be next. And I see Bette got married again. Good for her. I read it in the local paper."

"I wish we knew you were back here. Bette would've invited you."

Anabella shrugged her shoulders like it didn't matter to her and looked down. She studied her pale, crinkled hands with age spots. They were the only part of her body that seemed to be showing her age. After a long moment of silence, she very quietly said, "It's alright, Raquel. I came back to Brumby Flat with no expectations. I know some people will accept me back, and others won't be so kind. But Brumby Flat is my home and the memories I hold dear to me, out weight any negative feelings I may have. I believe I have made my peace with God."

"Well, that's good."

Raquel brought over to the table two cups of coffee, resting one on the table in front of Anabella.

"I heard about that poor woman in a coma. The model. The papers call it an attempted murder."

"They would, wouldn't they? The media thrives on this sort of thing. I think they'd like to see the title of murder town return to Brumby Flat."

"Well, it made the place so lively."

Anabella took a bite of her own homemade cupcake, with

no sign of hesitation or fear. Raquel watched her and finally took a cautious mouthful herself.

****

Phil Duncan had just returned to town, after visiting the city hospital. There was no change with Kitty Caulfield's condition according to her doctors and still no word from his Bali honeymooning wife.

He wasn't in a good frame of mind. As well as not being able to move forward on the Kitty situation, it was another anniversary of his hippy parents' mysterious disappearance. Before Duncan had turned eight years old, his parents decided to join a hitchhiking adventure tour to Tibet. They drove him up to Surfers Paradise to live with his mothers' straitlaced parents, Vivienne and Bert. That was the last time he saw them and with every passing year, he found it harder to remember what they had even looked like. They left in their Kombi van heading back to Sydney and were never heard from again. He was always sad whenever he thought about them.

He had to make an urgent pit stop at the local petrol station to fill up his car. The tall Nigerian couple were still running the business. Their English had improved a little.

He flipped the petrol cap open and started to fill up. He had spent over four hours on the road, so he was glad to get out and stretch his legs. As he stood stiffly there, another car pulled up on the other side of the petrol pump.

Out of the drivers' seat, she made her entrance unfurling her long legs. He tried hard not to look, but it was difficult not to notice her. She had auburn dyed shoulder length hair, framing pale blue-green eyes. But her legs seemed to go forever, under her black split skirt. She was wearing a wrap white T-shirt top with ruched sleeves to her elbows. She was definitely not a local. She started to fill up her car, the sunlight playing on her shiny auburn hair. Her eyes had a dreamy quality which was perfectly balanced by her small, pert nose and well-defined eyebrows. Her lips were wide and emphasised by the red berry gloss she had recently applied to them.

Geena Henderson leaned against her coal black convertible as she filled up, reflecting on her workday. She had just dropped into the Raindrops Shop to try and sell a range of her company's giftware. She found it very odd to find a shop full of water skis, snow skis, rain jackets, snow boots, gumboots and umbrellas in the middle of a region renown for long periods of drought. She had met Raquel who explained the current owner was away, but she did take her business card, a sales brochure and paid for a small selection of her goods. Raquel had chosen a trio of tea towels and an umbrella with galloping horses on them for herself and paid it in cash straight from the till. A sale was a sale and Geena was happy with that.

She had also visited the new Post Office further down the main street. The old building had been pulled down for the new town road which never happened. A new transportable room popped up on an empty block about six months ago, approved by local council. Bette was no longer running the Post Office from her shop. With enough work already on her plate, eighty-nine-year-old Mavis Dexter had stepped in and took on the job on a part time basis. Although her hands were riddled with arthritis, she had what she called a gummy leg and she forgot to wear her hearing aid most days, Mavis was hard working and very good with figures. She was also tech savvy, putting herself up on various dating websites with not much luck. A smear of rouge on her hollowed cheeks, her snow-white hair permed within an inch of its' life and her crinkled eyes with heavy blue eye shadow did nothing to persuade would be suitors to message her. But Geena got nowhere with her. Mavis was not interested in 'tourist trinkets' as she poetically called them.

Duncan studied Geena's long legs under his fair eyelashes, pretending to look at the gauge on the fuel pump. He followed the soft curves of her breasts noticing the small cluster of freckles there. She finished filling up her car before Duncan did. But he was more than happy to follow her inside, able to worship her legs from behind, undetected.

At the shop counter, she paid for the fuel and then asked them a question.

"I need to stay a night in the area. Is there a motel in this town?"

The couple didn't understand her, so Duncan jumped in to assist.

"Excuse me. Did you say you need accommodation for tonight?"

She turned at his deep, resonating voice and stared up into his bright blue eyes. She noticed how piercing they were, and how intense he looked behind his glasses.

She was standing so close; he could smell her sweet floral scented perfume.

"Yes, only for tonight. I'm a sales rep. I'm just passing through."

"Lucky, we bumped into each other. I have the only B&B

in town. Plenty of rooms. Quiet place with a half court tennis court and a pool. You can follow me."

"Oh wow, I am lucky, aren't I? To have found you." she fluttered her eyes at him and inched a little closer.

He cleared his throat, "I'm Phillip. Call me Phil."

She smiled, showing a small toothy gap, "Hello. I'm Geena."

He nodded and being a gentleman, he opened the shop front door for her.

She drove behind him up to the hill and when she hopped out of her car, she whirled around excitedly.

"Oh wow. You live here? It's lovely, quite a big house!" she exclaimed.

Duncan blushed inwardly.

"Yes, my wife and myself. Together we run this show."

Geena turned, "Oh, is she here too?"

"No, she's on holiday just at the moment," he said, adding, "It's you and just me."

"How much?"

"Only for tonight? Just fifty bucks is fine."

She smiled, "That's a very fair price for the service."

"It doesn't include breakfast."

"Oh, pity. It so should."

She headed around to the boot of her car, but Duncan beat her to it. As he went to remove her overnight bag, his hand lightly brushed across her bare right arm and she felt the electricity exchange between them. Her heart started to race inside her chest.

"Here. Let me take your bag for you."

"Thank you so much."

They entered through the kitchen back door of the house

and Duncan presented his temporary guest with the bank account details to pay for the night. He then led her upstairs straight to the last bedroom he had used.

"I hope you find it comfortable. There's a small bar fridge over there with milk and biscuits and the kettle is in the cupboard. Help yourself to coffee or tea. If you need anything, I'll be downstairs."

Geena studied her room, and nodded her head approvingly. He set her overnight bag down on the bed. Her eyes followed every movement he made. He knew she was watching him closely, but he tried to not read too much into it.

He closed the door gently behind him and trotted downstairs. He unlocked his and Bette's bedroom and removed his work laptop. He tucked it under his arm and went into their large lounge room with plush armchairs and standard lamps. Relaxing into his favourite armchair, he switched it on and started going through interview notes on the screen. He was quiet for a good hour. He finally scooped out his small flip notebook from his shirt pocket and started jotting down some notes. He circled three names on a lined page.

Phillip Proctor – invited guest

Reece Haddock – not at party

Dan Mundy – not at party

He then wrote 'to interview again.'

He studied the page for a minute, then added Anabella Williams to his list.

He spent another hour pouring over various reports and notes, and he added two more names to his suspect list. He sent a couple of text messages to Constable Steve Willaston.

Then he sat bolt upright when an awful thought hit him. The bedroom Geena had been offered, was the same bedroom Duncan had left his police issue handcuffs in one of the bedside drawers. He clicked his tongue and shook his head. He could leave it and hope his guest didn't rummage around and find it. Or he had to race upstairs and reclaim the handcuffs.

He decided on the second option and locking away his laptop, he rushed upstairs, taking two steps at a time. He stood at the bedroom door and checked his watch. It was only six o'clock in the afternoon so not too late to intrude on her.

He took a sharp intake of breath and then knocked firmly on the bedroom door.

Geena had been eagerly waiting for his return. She had already undressed and put on her dressing robe, soften her make up and freshen up in preparation. She had heard the wooden stairs creak. She turned and accidentally stubbed her left toe against the edge of the bed in her rush to look seductive. Limping slightly, she propped herself back on the floral bedcover and flicked her auburn hair back and then brushed it forward again.

"Come in," her voice called out. It sounded like a sultry invitation, so he entered the room hesitantly.

"Sorry to interrupt. I…I accidently left my tools of trade in your bedroom."

He found Geena reclined back on the bed with her back against the velvet headboard, wearing a red Chinese silk dressing robe. It clashed beautifully with her auburn hair. He felt himself blushing inwardly again and his cock was certainly showing signs of approval. He fought hard to control his reactions.

"You're too late," she said with a smirk, removing a set of handcuffs from the wide sleeve of her robe, "I found these and quite frankly, I am intrigued."

"I can explain. I am Detective Phillip Duncan. I can show you my ID."

"For real? You're a real detective," she giggled.

"Yes, I am."

She grinned at him, and with a sassy confident air, she clipped one end of the handcuffs to her right wrist and the other to the bed railing underneath the headboard before he had a chance to blink.

"So, am I under house arrest, Mister Officer?"

Duncan shook his head and put his hands on his hips, "Look, Geena. I am a married man, you know."

She winked back at him with a look of confidence, "Yes. I am a married woman too. But I want to. With you."

"Look. I don't think that we should..."

"What's the harm, Phillip? We are here alone. We aren't hurting anyone. My husband's not here, or your wife. One night of fun together. No one needs to know. Come on. How about it?"

He could feel his cock stirring. The lovely Geena was a little temptress. It had been a while since he had laid with and pleasured Bette. He hesitated for a minute, thinking about Bette but then realised she had left him, gone to Bali on her own. He had no idea what she was up to over there. It was doing his head in, just thinking about it. Geena was starting to become a welcome distraction for him.

His decision made, he crossed the room in a stride and pulled her down onto the bed, and a creamy breast with a sprinkle of freckles peeped out of the folds of her robe. She gasped as he sucked on her pink nipple and teased it with his expert tongue. He then stopped, looked down at her, finally noticing the fire breathing dragon tattoo on her left shoulder. He removed his glasses and started to undo his conservative pinstripe shirt. With her warm left hand, she undid the tie on her silk robe and parted her shapely pale legs to reveal her shaved pussy to him. He admired her offering. He could smell the sweet juices of her pussy.

"Well now!" he exclaimed. He slowly ran his forefinger along her naked right side which made her shiver under his slight, barely there touch. She closed her eyes and wondered what was coming next.

Now with shirt off, and his notebook in it safe, he propped up the shirt on a chair, and he went down on her. She strained her wrists against the cold steel handcuffs and arched her back as he held her hips and licked at her clitoris hungrily. She came screaming in waves of ecstasy soon after.

"Take me, Phillip. Fuck me, fuck me now, "she begged him, noticing the bulge in his trousers as he got up. She arched her back and put her knees up.

"Let's just stick to oral sex for now," he replied, unzipping his grey trousers. He let his pulsing erection unfurl and straddled the bed near her face, "Your turn now. Suck me."

After their oral sex session was over, he had the key for the handcuffs magically appear in his right hand and started to slowly release her and with his left hand, he held her chin and French kissed her. As soon as she was free of her shackles, she wrapped her lithe limbs around his naked torso and Duncan started to relax his emotional walls. He put aside his feelings of guilt and made love to her for hours. She responded by moving with him and changed positions willingly.

They lay back finally on the ravaged queen bed, hot and exhausted by their lustful exertions.

"What brought you out here again?" he asked after a few quiet minutes, wrapping her in his strong arms, and pulling her smooth freckled back against his chest.

"I work as a sales rep. I sell a range of giftware to shops. chemists, newsagents and shit like that. I travel all around the state. Sometimes, I have to travel interstate. It's funny, this is my first time here in Brumby Flat. I wasn't expecting to enjoy it half as much as I have."

He licked and nuzzled her exposed ear, "I'm so happy you came to Brumby Flat."

She giggled, "I am happy I met you too. Sorry but I have to go away in three hours. I haven't had a wink of sleep, thanks to you. Anyway. One day, I'll be back this way."

"Geena. You've made me feel alive."

"Doesn't your wife do that for you?"

He smiled tight lipped and whispered low in her ear, "Let's not talk about our married lives, okay? We should just live in the moments we have."

He turned her gently around to face him in bed and started to caress her lips, with a torrent of slow, intense and lingering kisses. She responded eagerly, her erect nipples pressing against his chest as the head of his hard cock expertly entered her and made her gasp.

Chapter Six

"Hello?" Raquel had picked up her mobile just in time. She was busy at work, dealing with yet another tablet dropped into a wine vat. She knew some of the wine makers and cellar hands were having affairs on the side, but she wished they would not madly chase each other around the laboratory spaces, the fermentation chambers and the underground wine cellar with such wild abandonment.

"Hey. It's me, girlie."

"Oh Phil. What is it? I'm working."

"My father has come here early. I can't drop what I'm doing. My hands are full of paint."

She sighed heavily, "And you think I can?"

He was quiet for a moment. "I know you finish work in five minutes. Look Sweetheart. I will make this up to you, I promise you. How about dinner this week or we go on a picnic somewhere real nice? He'll be at Adelaide airport in about ninety minutes. Please, please can you pick him up?"

"Okay, okay, but I expect to collect."

"Sure, girlie. His name is Will Proctor. And a heads up. He's a bit cranky. And he's hard of hearing. You'll have to talk a bit louder."

Ten minutes later, she jumped into her Pontiac and headed

down the highway. As she cruised at a hundred kilometres an hour, the dry landscape rushed by, huge gumtrees with twisted branches lining the road verge. Gradually the wide-open country spaces gave way to rows of neat little homes and shops. The threat of kangaroos, other wildlife and loose cows crossing the road had now vanished. The airport road came into view and she could see a plane coming into land in the distance. Raquel realised she would have to park in the expensive guest carpark area. Fortunately, she was running a bit late so she secretly hoped that Proctor's father had already collected his luggage from the baggage carousel, which would shorten the carpark stay. She found a parking spot between two huge petrol guzzling SUVs.

She rushed into the international airport terminal, nearly losing a shoe in the process. Her hair was up but had started to wilt in the heat, with strands falling against her face. Her navy dress was clinging to her and she could feel sweat under her armpits, but she had no time to freshen up. She stopped her march for a moment, wondering how she will ever find him in the busy airport. An idea hit her. She rushed up to the small newsagency booth in the foyer. She purchased a cheap magazine and a thick black texta. She flicked through the pages, found the palest advertisement page and scrawled 'Will Proctor' in large black letters all over it.

With magazine in hand, she walked over to the international arrivals area. She lifted the page up. A steady stream of travellers passed her by, some noticing her standing between taxi and uber drivers holding up marginally better signs.

Ten minutes passed before a tall elderly gentleman with a pair of snarly, narrow grey eyes stopped and glared at her. His peppery grey hair was cut short against his scalp and he was wearing a shabby polo neck jumper and old navy wool blend trousers. His thin lips twisted sideways, and he put down an oversized suitcase he was holding in his right hand. His voice was a growl and the accent was definitely Texan.

"I am Will Proctor. And who the hell are you?"

Raquel felt a lump rise in her throat and said sharply, "Sorry but your son was tied up with his silo work. He sent me to pick you up from the airport."

He squinted his eyes and made a low growling sound. "Okay. You're his squeeze."

"Well, no. Yes. Maybe I am. My name is Raquel. Please, call me Raquel."

He ignored her and charged right past her. For an elderly gent, she noticed he had quite a spring in his step. He then pointed down to his suitcase.

"It's heavy," he cautioned her. "Take some care with it."

She stared at him open mouthed. When she finally regained her composure, she walked calmly to the centre of the terminal to get one of those awkwardly large luggage trolleys. She knew his suitcase would weight a ton and she had no plans to damage her back carrying it.

When they finally got to her car, Will looked less than impressed. He had also removed his jumper, complaining about the dry heat to reveal a nineteen-seventies wide lapel shirt underneath.

"Alright," he muttered, "Is this the transport? It's a small vehicle. Goodness sakes. How am I going to fit? And with my luggage too."

"I'll make you, and it bloody fit," she whispered under her breath.

She wrestled with the car boot and after a few tries, she worked out the way to make his suitcase fit and the boot to close.

He banged his head bending to get into her car, so his mood did not improve. In fact, he complained all the way to Brumby Flat about the plane trip, the heat, the flies, the lack of air conditioning in her car and having insufficient leg room.

"God dammit. How long does it take to get there? My legs are practically curled over my head, girlie," he growled. She came to realise very quickly that to Phil Proctor 'girlie' was a term of endearment but when his father Will said it, it sounded like a slap in her face.

They arrived at Brumby Flat, just as the sun was starting to set so she quickly drove him up to the silos to show him Proctor's amazing mural of goats.

"My son is very talented," Will remarked, choking back his fatherly tears.

"Yes, he is," she had to agree with him. Busloads of tourists arrived every week to admire his work.

She was glad to get home. She quickly showed him around the cottage and then disappeared into their bedroom. When Proctor returned later in the evening, he found Raquel curled up in their bed, reading a fantasy novel. He nodded his head when her eyes looked up and he closed the door very quietly behind him. He could tell right away that she was not in the mood to communicate. He walked back to the dining room and continued his catch up with his father. He was happy hearing all the news of home.

****

The morning light was spreading its warm golden glow slowly across the dry landscape. A rooster could be heard crowing in the far distance and the laughing of kookaburras echoed from high in nearby gumtrees.

He seemed unperturbed by some of the strange wildlife noises around him. Will Proctor chomped away blissfully on his sizeable Cuban cigar. He was blowing out smoke through his dentures and rustled the local newspaper he was reading on the front veranda of Phil's cottage. His eyes were sharp so he could read the small print easily enough. His hearing was quite another matter entirely.

"God dammit. There's nothing in this goddamn paper to read. Doesn't anything happen in this town?" he growled loudly to himself. Proctor's adopted cattle dog Maxine had planted herself at his feet.

Raquel walked out at that precise moment, cradling a cup of hot chocolate she had made for herself. She had her robe tied over her underwear. She saw Will too late, perched on a deck chair, with a cushion stuck under his bony old bum. She decided she was forced to brave the great outdoors with him inside it.

"How are you?" she leaned over him and raised her voice at him.

He blinked up at her, "Yeah, okay. I'm really fine. How's my son's squeeze today?"

Her neck hairs bristled, "Please don't call me that. I am very nice to you."

"Ah, grow some balls. This ain't no Disney pixie land fairy tale that you're swanning around in," he growled back.

She smiled, "Oh yes, I definitely know that. I know it too well. It's a nice day on the veranda."

He snorted, "This is a goddamn porch where I come from. Don't you Aussies speak God's English in this country?"

"Man, you sure are a bitchy old thing," she said under her breath as she sipped her hot chocolate slowly.

"What are your plans today, Will?" she shouted at him, half glad to, "Do you want me to show you around the town maybe?"

He glared at her, "Listen girlie, nothing you got in this town would excite me. Sure, I've seen everything, being from Texas and all."

"Okay, well, the McCarthy's down the road have invited you over for a barbeque later this afternoon. They own the black mare your son rides. They called me about fifteen minutes ago to specially invite you over, Will."

"Man, I love a good old-fashioned Texas barbeque. Tell them I'll be over for sure. What time, girlie?"

"Lunchtime, about twelve."

"Fine. Tell them I'm coming. I'll show them how to make a real barbeque."

Raquel smiled slightly and took another sip of her hot chocolate, "I am sure you will."

She looked down at Maxine, who was lying on the porch, her eyes focused on Will. Raquel shook her head, thinking that bloody dog likes everyone.

"Some watchdog you *are*," she muttered. Maxine just blinked and looked at her with big brown eyes. Then she wagged her bushy tail across the porch.

****

The McCarthy's place was a good kilometre away from

Proctor's cottage but Will insisted he would walk the distance. While Will started his long walk, Raquel headed off to the local post office. She had just received a text message from Mavis, saying her latest parcel had arrived for pick up.

She charged down the dirt road in her Pontiac and when she entered the main street, she pulled over before the post office came into sight. She had a double take moment. She tooted her horn, certain she could see her friend Bette walking along, across the road near the Brumby Flat Secondary School. Actually, she was not walking, she was balancing on the small brick fence near the school front office, which amused Raquel. Bette looked up and smiled broadly, waving back. Then she hopped off the fence and ran across the road, not looking to check for traffic. Fortunately, Brumby Flat was a relatively quiet small town.

"Hey doll," Bette put her arms on the driver's side window, leaning in, "Good to see you again."

Raquel shrugged her shoulders and exclaimed, "Wow, you're back. I thought you were still sunning yourself in Bali."

"No. I came back last night. I am not happy, doll, not happy."

"What's wrong now?"

"I think the love of my life has been fooling around," she said with a smirk which genuinely shocked Raquel. Bette looked far too calm if it was true.

"Bloody hell. Are you drunk?"

Bette burst into a fit of giggling, "Ah, doll. I might be. I had half a bottle of gin this morning. But I don't care. I've come back home to get my heart broken, looks like it."

Her friend was about to ask what made her believe

Duncan had been unfaithful, when a voice echoed from across the road. Bette whirled around.

Assumed to be a teacher, the man with peppered grey hair and a short reddish beard approached them. He was not very tall and was dressed in a tight navy suit which did not hide his pronounced pot belly. As he came closer, Bette noticed his deep-set hazel eyes and nose. He didn't look angry as his lips were curved up in a half smile. He reached them and looking directly at Bette, he said in a strong voice of authority, "I saw what you were doing, trespassing on school property. I see you haven't changed. I remember who you are."

She knitted her eyebrows together and it took a minute before a lightning bolt hit her.

"It's you. Oh my god. It's really you!" she exclaimed.

He winked back and added, "You have some free time for a quick catch up? We can talk about your continued and damned obvious disrespect for authority."

Raquel piped up in the driver's seat, "Hey. What's going on?"

Bette turned back to her, "Look doll, I'll catch up with you later on. I promise. I am just going to catch up with an old acquaintance."

"Okay. Well, don't forget we haven't finished that conversation," Raquel started her car and drove off slowly, giving Bette a little wave.

Bette felt a little flustered and smiled at the teacher who was only slightly taller than she was, "Mr. Haddock, isn't it?"

He nodded his head, hands on hips, flashing a toothy smile behind the beard,

"Good memory. It's been more than twenty years."

"You remember my name?"

"Oh yes, of course I do, Bette Chiffley. I have a good memory too for all the kids I've taught. Or in your case, kids I have tried to teach. Actually, I recall you were better than most of them."

He steered her across the road, loosely holding her left elbow, looking out for road traffic. He opened the front door of school reception and led her to his office in the main school building, past the perplexed reception staff. She pointed to the signage on his door.

"Yes, I am the school principal."

"Wow, you were just a maths teacher back at high school."

He chuckled. "Yes, just one of those. I worked hard. I worked my arse to the top."

Bette nudged her elbow gently in his ribs, "Well, if Brumby Flat is the best place to be, I am really happy for you."

She turned her head at the sound of loud, screaming voices outside his office window.

He smiled, "It's okay. Just morning recess."

He indicated for her to take a seat as he settled into his impressive leather office chair behind his desk. She stopped in the middle of the office to admire his bookcase of maths books and classic novels. Then she stared at his framed diplomas on the side wall.

"Oh wow. Impressive," she said, sitting down finally.

He shuffled a few papers to the right side of his desk and continued his story since they last met, "Brumby Flat Secondary School is okay. It was not where I wanted to start my career as a principal but it could've been worse maybe. The kids here are great and the parents are more of a challenge. Everyone has the perfect angel you know, or the most gifted child. Now, I was a teacher at the school for another five years after you left. After that, I taught at a couple of high schools along the southeast coast. I remember you were friends with Magda and…there was another young lady at school?"

"Mandy-Jane," she corrected him, "Mandy-Jane Fischer."

"Oh yes, and Magda became a well-known fashion model. I wasn't surprised, given her looks and sass at school. Changed her name, didn't she?"

"Yes, to Kitty Caulfield."

"Well, you haven't changed at all Bette Chiffley. Still testing authority, I see. I recall you got into trouble a couple of times at high school."

She giggled, "Just for little things. I was caught smoking a ciggie once, behind the gym."

She started to hiccup and placed her right palm over her mouth. "Oh, I'm sorry. Pardon me."

Mr. Haddock leaned forward on his desk, his hands clasped into a steeple and finally noticed she was swaying a little in the chair.

"Are you drunk, Bette Chiffley?"

"Pardon me. Yes sir. I believe I am. But I am not a schoolgirl anymore. You can't reprimand me."

He smiled, "That's true. However, you are in a school and please, call me Reece. So, let's pretend nothing is wrong. You haven't had a drink."

She started to cry, a few tears trailing down her lightly powdered cheeks, "I can't pretend anymore."

Mr. Haddock grabbed a box of tissues from his top desk drawer and pushed it directly under her nose, "Here. Wipe away your tears, tell me all about it. What brought you here to Brumby Flat?"

She blew her nose and dabbed at her large blue jay eyes, "I'm sorry that I'm a bit emotional. I haven't seen you in over twenty years and look at me. I start crying like a basket case. Well, I just got married last month."

"Congratulations."

"No, no" she sniffed and wiped her nose, "It's not good at all. I love my new husband madly but he's all work, work, work. Completely consumed by his work. It defines him."

"I see. So, what does your fellow do for a crust?"

"He's a Detective. Detective Phillip Duncan. Maybe you've heard of him."

Mr. Haddock stiffened up in his chair, "The name sounds familiar."

"Before I married Phillip, I was married to someone else. I pretty much married soon after finishing high school. My first husband was Sandy Mitchell. We moved over here from Tasmania to start a franchise business. I own The Raindrops Shop in town. You might've heard about the Brumby Flat murders?" Mr. Haddock nodded and she continued, "It was more than a couple of years ago now, but my Sandy ended up being the serial killer. It was a great, huge shock to me, I can tell you. He went to jail and I got a divorce as soon as I could get it. Phillip very kindly helped me through everything, the darkness around me."

He shook his head and clapped his hands together," Bette, that's incredible. You've married good and pure evil."

"Not by choice, Reece."

"Sometimes, life presents interesting twists. I have to be candid with you, but I had serious misgivings about coming to live and work in this small town. Because of its bloody reputation but then I realised that kids are kids, wherever they are, and they need, well, they have a right to a good education. So, I put the kids first and my career obviously came next. I have been here for three months now, so I think I'm well over my fears. I like the town."

Bette nodded her head. "Yes, I understand. Glad you did. Oh, before I forget, Kitty Caulfield is here in Adelaide, you know."

Mr. Haddock nodded and looked serious. "Yes. I read about what happened to her. It's been all over the media. Poor girl. I hope she recovers."

"Unfortunately, it happened at our wedding reception. A guest found her at the dam unconscious. It was horrible and the whole situation brought back terrible memories for me. I don't know if you remember Mandy-Jane…"

Mr. Haddock cut her off in midsentence, "I remember the murder investigation and the news reports. She was found in a dam, wasn't she? Her body was found, I mean."

"Yeah, well, not exactly. It was a reservoir where they found her body."

He glanced down at his expensive wristwatch and brushed a forefinger over his beard, "I'm sorry Bette. Run out of time. Duty calls me in five minutes. It's Friday and I have to visit one of the classes. I like to do this once a week and interact with the kids. Today I'm attending an art class which should be interesting. Maybe we have some undiscovered Rembrandts. One can only hope."

He winked at her playfully.

"Of course."

Bette stood up and clutched the back of the chair suddenly. For a moment, the room seemed to be spinning around her, but she recovered very quickly. As she turned to leave, she noticed a few framed photographs hanging right next to his diplomas. She moved a couple of steps closer to admire them.

One was a photograph of Reece Haddock standing with a group of other teachers she presumed. The second one showed Haddock with a group of school students gathered around a large footy trophy. However, it was the third photograph that proved to be of the most interest to her.

Haddock was smiling straight at the camera, on his left was a schoolgirl also looking front and centre. But next to him, standing on his right was Mandy-Jane Fischer in her brief uniform smiling, looking straight up at Haddock. She immediately recognised her friend's punk style light brown hair, the black leather choker around her neck and the dark, smudged eye makeup that she always wore. It was Mandy-Jane or else her dead ringer.

"Oh wow. There she is, in a photo!" she exclaimed excitedly.

Mr. Haddock shifted awkwardly back in his leather chair, making it creak, "I'm sorry? What is it?"

She pointed to her best friend in the photograph, "It's Mandy-Jane, right there. I can't believe it's her."

He shrugged his broad shoulders, "Oh. I didn't know who it was…it was so long ago. It's just a nice memory of the first school I taught at, straight after teachers' college."

Bette listened carefully to the lack of emotion in his voice, knitted her brows together and then looked back at him with a partial smile, "Oh yes. Of course. It was over twenty years ago."

"Well, the simple fact is she wasn't in any of my classes.

Sorry, I honestly don't remember what she looked like. I don't even remember who took the photo or when it was taken. I had no idea it was her."

"No matter. It was a nice surprise to see her again. I do miss her."

"It was good to see you again, Bette. I hope your new marriage works out for you. You have to give each other a fighting chance. It's early days yet."

"Thanks Reece, take care of yourself."

She closed the door behind her.

When she had gone, Reece Haddock leaned forward. He rested both elbows on his desk, ran his hands through his peppered grey hair and stared point blank at the third photograph on his wall.

"Fuck," he said under his breath, "Fuck, fuckety, fuck."

He rummaged in the lost and found box located next to his desk and then threw a pencil case across the room, which clipped the edge of the bookcase.

One of the reception staff knocked, then opened his door slowly and peered in.

"Are you okay, Reece? I heard a really loud noise," she said. She was a matronly lady with a plain round face under frizzy dyed orange hair and with a rounder body to match. She took far too much interest in him, but he was okay with that.

He nodded his head. "I'm alright, Sharon. I'll be off to that art class in a few minutes. How's the head lice breakout going? I believe there's ten year eight kids affected so far. A very unfortunate situation."

Chapter Seven

Old Will Proctor strode down the main street of Brumby Flat with the midday sun high in the sky. He didn't have the sexy swagger of his son, but he was certainly agile for his age. He preferred to walk around rather than drive. He was wearing his old mustard coloured skivvy and well-worn navy trousers with patches on the knees. He topped off his day's outfit with a battered old fishing hat. His back was only slightly hunched at his shoulders, which also showed his advanced age. At his heels, Maxine was panting and bouncing along, tail wagging. She was hanging around him, mainly because he was around more often than her owners were.

His tawny gnarled right hand plunged into his hip back pocket to bring out a couple of tatty envelopes to post back to Texas before he entered the local Post Office. He told Maxine to sit still and wait outside.

Mavis Dexter looked up from the front counter over her prescription eyeglasses when she heard the door slam shut behind him, from a sudden hot burst of wind. Her grey crinkled eyes narrowed and then widened as she recognised Will Proctor. She was glad that she had remembered to powder her nose and had smeared some rouge on her hollowed, crinkled cheeks that morning. There weren't many men in town close to her own age that could walk and talk so freely. She had God to thank for the appearance of Will Proctor in Brumby Flat.

Unfortunately, neither of them liked wearing their hearing aids so conversation wasn't always easy.

"Hello, my darling Mavis," Will shouted at her and tipped his hat in her direction.

"Oh Will, it's so nice to see you again," she smiled, her new perfect snow-white dentures on show.

He learnt against the counter, a mix of Old Spice and mothballs and passed over the envelopes to her.

"They're post marked for Texas."

Mavis blushed and took the letters from him, "Oh Will, I'll mail these off for you right away."

"Say Ma'am, what's to do at night in this town?"

She strained to hear him and replied with undisguised enthusiasm, "Take me out for a night on the town? How lovely of you. Of course, yes, I'll go."

Will squinted his eyes and nodded his head, believing he had heard her response,

"Nothing in this town? No, you say? Well, that's just too bad. I thought the hotel is open tonight. Dinner at six, isn't it?"

Mavis blushed again and patted her snow white tightly permed hair, "Oh, you want dinner and sex too? Oh Will, you've a very naughty man." She giggled away like a young girl.

Will wagged his thin bony forefinger at her, "Darling, I'm not fifty, I'm a bit older than that."

"Meet you at six-thirty tonight? At the pub? Well, okay."

He smiled at her one more time and then tipped his hat,

"Good night to you, ma'am."

He raised his voice and this time, she heard him.

"See you later, Will Proctor."

When he had left, she took out her compact and viewed her face, her arthritic right-hand trembling.

"Well, well Mavis old girl, you got yourself a hot date tonight," she muttered proudly to herself.

While she rejoiced within the walls of the transportable Post Office, Phil Proctor was busy entertaining his own date in a quiet paddock, a good kilometre away.

He expertly popped a cork on a champagne bottle and leaned over the picnic blanket to fill Raquel's lifted glass to the brim.

"Why girlie, you look in shock," he mused in his low Texan drawl.

Raquel shrugged her shoulders and lay back on the only patch of green grass in the paddock, "I am. I wasn't expecting to really go on a picnic with you. It's been really nice. But I am full."

"Well, I am a man of my word," he winked at her, under his Akubra. "You did me a great favour. Picking up my old man Will from the airport. Damn grateful to you. You deserve a picnic in our own backyard. Here's to good health and happiness."

"Yep. Mud in your eye."

They clinked their glasses together in a toast and Proctor also lay back, propped up on his right elbow, his long legs unfurling across the blanket.

"It's McCarthy land. Are you sure they won't mind us being here?"

"Relax, darling. We're all good friends around here."

He stared at her, his eyes roving over her body with no hint of shame, "You know how damn pretty you look today?"

"You're welcome to explain."

But she knew she looked good. He gave her notice early in the morning about the picnic lunch so she had plenty of time to prepare. She ran a warm lavender bath at home and she put on her sexiest wrap dress with a side split down her curvy right leg. Her hair was tied up in a sleek ponytail and her face makeup was applied light with a thin blue pencil line over her eyelids.

He nodded and removed his hat. "Well okay, let's see. You have the prettiest eyes. And you look so damn hot in your tight little dress there. I am very sorry that I am staring at you the way I am, but I can't rightly help myself, ma'am."

He changed his position and moved closer to her, crossing his legs. He took a long swig of champagne and dropped the empty glass on the dirt ground beside him.

"You're sounding very poetic today," she remarked.

"I am telling you what's true. You're a beautiful lady. And I really wish..." his voice trailed off.

"Phil. What do you wish for?"

To answer her, he rubbed his warm right hand over her right leg, up to her thigh. Then his hand disappeared under the folds of her wrap dress. She closed her eyes and took a sharp intake of breath as he successfully found and concentrated his efforts on her clitoris. She parted her thighs slightly, enjoying his light, well-practised touch.

"Phil," she breathed his name, "You shouldn't do that."

"Why? I can see you are enjoying it. I really wish we could go back in time, to when we first met. But I know there's no chance. Hey. Why don't we go back to the truck, girlie. There's something I'd really like to do."

He took his hand away slowly. She straightened her dress and noticed the strong look of desire in his blue eyes and the bulge in the tight crotch of his stone washed jeans. But something else had caught her eye as well. She was squinting against the glare of the sun and shaded her eyes with her right hand so she could take a better look. She could see a large black shape in the distance, at the top of the hill behind Proctor.

"Phil, is there something else in the paddock? With us?"

He smiled and winked at her, "Maybe there's a cow or sheep. A 'roo?"

She shook her head and pointed up the hill, "No. It looks like a bloody big bull to me. I think…it's seen us too."

Proctor turned his head around and saw the huge black creature trotting down the hill, swinging its huge set of horns. He immediately leapt up to his feet and grabbed up the picnic blanket and started throwing the plastic dishes into the basket. The champagne glasses were chucked in as well and clinked together a second time.

"Hell. You're right. It's a goddamn bull. We gotta get out of here. Quick smart."

"Shit. The gate must be four hundred metres back," Raquel gasped, brushing grass off her dress.

"No time, girlie, no time. We'd better head straight to the fence and jump it."

"What? Climb? In my good dress?"

He grabbed her right hand firmly and pulled her forward, the picnic basket swinging in his other. As they ran for the fence, the bull started to gallop down the hill. Proctor turned his head back a couple of times to make sure there was enough distance between them and the animal.

When they arrived at the wire fence, Proctor dropped the picnic basket over it and his hat blew off into the paddock. He looked back again, and he could nearly see the eyes of the beast barrelling down on them, so he ignored the lost Akubra and half lifted Raquel onto the top of the fence.

"You right? Can you make it down by yourself?" he asked, barely taking a breath.

She nodded and pulled the dress around the top of her thighs. She found her footing over the other side. She was thankful that she had worn flat shoes for the picnic.

Proctor then followed her, taking one big step up and he sprung himself over the fence like a man half his age. He didn't quite make it over without getting a small scrape. The tip of a horn tore a small patch from the seat of his jeans.

Safely over, he grabbed her hand again and scooped up the dropped picnic basket and ran. He only stopped when they were a good five metres away from the paddock boundary.

The bull was now trotting up and down the fence line, snorting. He had stopped at the fence and shook his large, wide black head with two enormous curved horns at the end of it.

"He might be a friendly bull, "Raquel said.

"I doubt it. Look what he did to my jeans. Lost my best hat too, but never mind. He's welcome to it," he replied. He turned around and showed his backside.

Raquel giggled and gently patted his bum where the piece was missing, "Well, at least you're not hurt. You have to admit that was fun. Escaping a wild paddock bull."

He laughed and suddenly grabbed her waist, pulling her up against him.

"Yeah, my sweetheart. Come on."

He threaded his fingers through hers and guided her towards the direction of his pickup truck.

She smiled up at him, shielding her eyes from the bright sun with her free hand, "Phil, what are you up to?" she asked him.

He turned to her as they stood in front of the truck. He dropped the picnic basket. They stood there in a small clearing, surrounded by a canopy of tall, narrow gum trees and low shrubs. The sky was a pale blue above them, and wild birds sang their songs to them from high in the trees.

Proctor very tenderly clutched the sides of her bare arms and stared into the depths of her soul. She shivered under his firm, familiar touch.

Without another word exchanged between them, he leaned over and kissed her. Raquel pulled back a little, but his lips were greedy and persistent. His tongue danced in her mouth. Proctor took her as a helpless prisoner. She responded and kissed him back eagerly. She moaned deep in her throat as his breath came hot and heavy against her neck as he traced his fore finger over the curve of a creamy breast. He reached into her dress top to bare an erect, heaving nipple to the elements. The shoulder strap of her dress came down to bare her shoulder as well. With his other hand, he thrust it under her wrap dress. His hand lingered between her warm thighs and pushed down on her panties. They slipped unwanted onto the dry, dirt ground. A finger disappeared inside her, playing with her clitoris. Raquel audibly gasped and leaned her back against the grill of the pickup truck. She was enjoying his intimate touching of her. She could even forgive him for removing parts of her clothing for access to pleasure her.

Then he easily lifted her onto the bonnet of his truck. She sat there, her right breast exposed to the sun and her thighs slightly apart. He quickly unzipped his jeans, looking straight at her, admiring her body as he did. His cock unfurled to its' full satisfying size.

Proctor pulled her legs gently down, and parted them wider. He lunged forward and thrust his cock slowly and deep into her wet pussy. She felt his thick cock fill her up like a refreshing drink. There was a delightful smacking sound as her pussy lips completely enveloped his penis. She closed her hazel eyes and arched her back on the bonnet and gasped as he continued to hammer her. It was gentle at first but as the pressure to release his own pleasure grew, his thrusting became stronger inside her and at a much faster pace. He clutched and kneaded her bare breast with his left hand, and he held her waist with his right. She screamed as he successfully exploded inside her and he cried out her name. She smiled, enjoying the warm sensation between her thighs.

Proctor leaned over her and sucked on her bare nipple after.

"Are you okay, girlie?" he breathed.

She simply nodded. After a few quiet minutes, she flipped the folds of her wrap dress over to cover up her modesty and Proctor offered his hand to help her down off the truck bonnet. On level ground, they searched into each other's eyes, and then their lips gently touched and kissed.

As they drove back to his cottage in silence, her hand rested gently on his left knee.

****

Bette Duncan had invited Raquel the next evening to dine with her at the local Fetlock and Spur Hotel.

She opened her wardrobe to work out what to wear. Raquel had not been inside the hotel for well over a year and she had to make sure that she looked her best. She chose to wear a floral maxi dress with a deep V-neck and billowing sleeves. She teamed the dress with a string of fake pearls. It was a look she knew Anabella Williams would no longer approve of. She refreshed her eye makeup in the bathroom mirror and walked undetected past Proctor and his father Will in the lounge, fighting over the evening's television programming. She drove down to the pub.

On the exterior, the town's only hotel looked the same but when Raquel stepped inside the dining room, the interior had shed it's dark and gloomy dimness. Suddenly there was plenty of shimmer, light and sparkle. The cheap plastic chairs were now covered in gold trimmed seat covers, the tables were square and made of solid wood and covered with gold flecked tablecloths. The surrounding walls were now painted a pale peach and a decorative border trim of florals and gold ribbons adorned the cornices of the ceiling. The dim old light fittings were now removed and replaced with three amazing eight globe crystal chandeliers which reflected all the vivid new colours in the room. The dining area was full of people and there was a line up at the bar, ordering meals and drinks. Behind the bar, was a huge glass mural of horses galloping across a dry plain with the full name of the pub embossed over the image. But the locals just called it 'The Fetty.'

When her eyes had finally adjusted to the brightness of the new lighting, she saw Bette wave to her from a table in the far-right corner. Bette got up to welcome her friend, looking radiant in a light linen shirt matched with black pants.

Raquel raced up smiling and took the spare seat.

"I can't believe how much the pub's changed!" she exclaimed.

Bette nodded, handing her an authentic leatherbound menu. "When Brumby Flat had the reputation of a 'murder' town, the hotel was busy and obviously it's stayed that way. The menu is the same, schnitzels, pork sausages and fish and chips. But they have added Chicken Kiev to the menu. That's new."

"Nice. Fish and chips it is."

She closed the menu and put it aside on the table.

"How's Phil Proctor's father?"

"He's hard work. He doesn't like me and I know he knows what I'm thinking about him. He's as independent as hell. It was bloody funny today."

"What happened?"

"The McCarthy's invited him over to their farm for barbeque lunch. He came back very unhappy. Said was expecting barbeque steak and got really burnt, skinny lamb chops instead. Kept calling their place 'over at the ranch'."

Bette chuckled, then looked serious.

"Well then. Time for my news. Look at this. I found this note tucked under a pillow, in one of the bedrooms upstairs. It's signed 'Genie.'"

She waved the small piece of paper under Raquel's nose. She then slipped the paper back into her purse.

"Like Genie in a bottle?"

"Doll, you're not taking me very seriously, are you?"

"Well, what does this note say?"

"Seriously. Thank you for a great time, it says!" she exclaimed. "Now what does that tell you? I confronted him with the note but he avoided all my questions. I think he's gone and had an affair. He had just one guest while I was away. They shacked up for the night, I'm pretty sure of it."

"But you might be wrong. Maybe the guest really enjoyed their stay," her friend said quietly.

"Look at what I went through with Sandy Mitchell. I don't want my new husband to cheat on me. Yet again."

"In his defence, he didn't know what you were doing over there in Bali."

"Oh my god. Whose side are you bloody on? I thought you were my friend!" Bette exclaimed.

"I don't think…I'm not siding with anyone. I am just saying it's very easy to jump to conclusions. If you get this wrong, your marriage might be over. Before it even begins."

"It's already finished and over with. I am done. I think I have no option but to annul this marriage. I will tell Phillip tomorrow of my decision."

"Bette, you can't be serious…"

Suddenly, Raquel flinched when she felt someone's stray elbow accidentally poke her back. She glanced around and finally realised the hotel had filled up with even more locals. The bar had a line-up of men holding beers around it and each chair at the dining tables was now filled.

"What's going on?" she asked Bette.

"Entertainment's on tonight. Always draws a crowd but this one, I think it will go off with a bang."

Raquel scanned the bar one more time. She hadn't seen some of the local farmers for ages and then she spotted him. He stood out in his smart burgundy suit and white shirt, against a sea of rugged men in flannel shirts. His brown eyes shone bright in a strong, tanned face framed with wavy sandy hair. He had a strong square jawline. Clean shaven and lean in body, he was standing there, leaning against the bar cradling a glass of red wine. He was certainly no farmer. The rest of them were clutching their cold beers.

"Wow. Who's that?" she nodded, "The talent at the bar? The guy in the suit."

"Him? That's the new local real estate agent. He moved into town about a month ago, doll. You're a bit slow to notice the hot new talent."

"Okay. He's pretty hot looking. Is he single? Do you know much about him?"

Bette heaved a sigh. "I believe he is single. His name is Sullivan O'Grady. I don't know anything else. But I'm sure that's what you wanted to know next. He's younger than us so you shouldn't even be looking, doll."

"He's not sucking on a lollipop and skipping around the dining room, so I don't think he's too young at all."

"What about Phil Proctor?"

Raquel shrugged her shoulders, "What about him? Look, you're not the only one around with man issues. But I'm not in the right frame of mind to talk about it right now. I just want to meet our Mr. Sullivan over there."

"Alright then, it's easy. We'll just walk over to the bar and you chat to him. Oh, maybe not now. Looks like the entertainment's starting," Bette had stood up but quickly sat down again.

A petite lady with a long blonde plait cascading down her back had appeared in front of the pool table at the rear of the dining room and when she did, the music stopped playing over the speakers. The crowd hushed in anticipation. She was dressed as an Arabian princess, her pretty oval face with pale blue eyes peeped out behind a fine pink veil. She wore a brief two-piece fuchsia pink costume which showed off her perfectly flat belly and small pert breasts.

Some guy at the bar yelled out, "Yeah, alright!"

She started to elegantly turn and twist her pale hands and limbs and began a slow belly dance rolling motion. With an elegant slender forefinger, she pressed the 'on' button of her portable stereo system on the pool table next to her. An exotic middle eastern song echoed across the dining room and she moved with a spirited elegance to it. Her face smiled in pleasure as she moved her curvaceous hips seductively and surrendered to the rhythm of the melodic music. She slowly turned around a couple of times, inviting the audience in the room to focus on her and believe she only had eyes for them.

Then she bent over, shapely legs spread apart and opened a large wicker basket from underneath the pool table. She carefully drew out a writhing, chunky diamond python which measured as long as she was tall. There was an audible gasp arising from the audience and two women went screaming and running through the dining tables and straight outside.

The performer placed the snake over her head and as if on cue, the python wound its' way around her hips and glided along her pale right arm. She gyrated to the music again as the snake weaved around her body. She danced suggestively, adding the elegant positioning of her wrists to her portrayal of a beguiling muse. She stopped again and bent over another large wicker basket. This time, she pulled out a smaller golden hued python with bright red ruby eyes. She placed it over her head and instead of heading down to hug her body, the reptile stayed draped around her neck and shoulders.

She started her seductive dance again, the snakes roving freely around her lithe body. As she continued her performance, one of the women returned from outside, persuaded by her former husband who said in a gruff voice, "What's your problem. love? It's just a snake. Snakes are everywhere in the bush."

The experienced snake dancer shimmed down onto her knees and arched her back. She slowly bent her head as far back as she could comfortably go and used her small, pale hands to create an elegant dance. The snakes seemed to know their place through the dance routine, and did not interfere with her fluid movements. She then rose again slowly and continued her belly dance, her trim torso rippling at amazing speed.

Raquel leant forward and whispered in Bette's ear, "Wow this is different."

Her friend nodded and glanced down at her mobile phone, "Shit. It's my Phil calling. I'll take this outside. Be right back."

Outside, away from eager listening ears, Bette was less than kind or diplomatic to her husband, "What is it now?" she hissed into her mobile phone.

There was a few seconds' silence before he answered, "When are you coming home? We are long overdue for a talk, my love."

"Listen Phil. Do you think you can talk your way out of the last two weeks? Maybe we rushed into this stupid marriage."

"Bette honey, you're being a bit over dramatic. Come home and let's talk it over."

"No. I'll come back when I'm ready. I'll divorce you as soon as possible."

"Bette. Come on. Give us half a chance. I love you and that's why I asked you to marry me in the first place. Come back now and let's put the cards on the table."

"No. Maybe. I'll think it over."

She turned off her mobile to stop his calls and text messages. She went back into the hotel dining room and noticed the performance was over. The noise level had increased, and people were freely walking around the tables.

Coming up to their table, she noticed Raquel was not there. She turned her head at the pleasant sound of familiar laughter and realised her friend had relocated to the bar, leaning in and chatting animatedly to Mr. O'Grady. He seemed to be mirroring her body language too.

By the time Raquel returned to their dining table, the plates of food had arrived and Bette was already halfway through her meal. She was wolfing her food down like she hadn't eaten for days. Usually, Bette ate very lightly.

"Sorry about that. I got to talk with the real estate guy Sullivan. He's really nice."

"Yes, so I noticed, doll. You looked like you were getting along."

Raquel sighed and flicked her head to one side, "Well, yeah. I think he likes me. I have been invited to his office next Friday for a coffee. I didn't say I would go. I'll see what happens next."

"Playing with fire, you are. What about Phil Proctor?"

"What about Duncan?"

Bette fluttered her big, blue jay eyes, "Yes, I get it, doll. Mine wants to discuss things but I don't want to. It's not easy.

Tonight, I'm going to stay away in the big smoke. Now, there's something else I needed to talk to you about. It's about Reece Haddock."

"Who?"

"He was that guy I was talking to at the school. Let me explain…"

****

Bette was driving along the highway, away from Brumby Flat, heading to the city. Duncan had invited her over to their home to discuss their relationship but she was not prepared to listen. She had already made up her mind that their marriage was over anyway.

She was not accustomed to driving at night. The dark landscape flashed past, the road ahead grey and pock marked with small bumps and potholes. She was happy not to see the dry brittle fields she knew were out there. She found the idea of a new drought looming in the region an extremely depressing prospect. It would affect sales of umbrellas, rain wear and snow gear in her shop.

A car was coming from the opposite direction and at the last minute, she remembered to dip her headlights.

As she drove her car on ahead, with high beams switched back on and coasting along at one hundred kilometres an hour, she had not noticed the giant road train bearing down at a rapid speed behind her. She only realised it was there when its impatient driver honked loudly and their high beams flashed in her eyes. The intense lights were reflected from the rear-view mirror.

She immediately turned down her car radio.

"What the fuck," she said aloud, shading her eyes, trying desperately to see the open road ahead. They honked behind her again and this time it looked like the front grill of the truck was ready to roll over the rear of her car.

She was forced to speed up to hundred and ten kilometres to clear the truck. She settled into the new speed, hoping there wasn't a police trap somewhere ahead.

But the driver lunged the rig forward again and Bette saw the movement through her rear-view mirror. The road ahead was dark and a kangaroo could hop out onto the road anytime. But Bette knew she had no choice but to take the risk. She pressed her foot hard down on the accelerator and her Holden responded. In a matter of a few seconds, her car hit the speed of one hundred and thirty kilometres, and she managed to put some distance between her car and the road train.

"Who is that bloody idiot?" she exclaimed loudly, shaking her head. She was going to switch the car radio back on but decided against it. The truck still had its high beams on which made it difficult for Bette to see the road ahead of her.

After a minute of driving at the higher speed, she started to ease her foot off the accelerator and began to relax a little. The blinding lights of the high beams seemed to have disappeared. She thought the truck must have turned down a side road. She looked ahead now, rather than behind, relieved she had lost the rude, impatient truck driver.

Suddenly, she heard a loud horn blast behind her which made her jump and the rig was now right at the rear of her car, bearing down on her again. This time, their front headlights were not switched on, so the rig had actually crept up on her. Then they flashed her with the high beams, nearly blinding her. She felt a slight bump and was sure that the truck had connected with her rear bumper.

Trying to outrun the heavy vehicle had not worked so she frantically thought of another alternative. She sped up again and looked for a wide verge far ahead. She planned to pull over and stop safely, letting the truck pass. She decided it was not worth going to the city anymore. She planned to turn around and drive straight home after she found a safe place to stop.

Once again, she managed to place some distance between her car and the road train. Rounding a bend in the road, she saw her opportunity to escape the escalating situation. She remembered there was a wide gravel verge before a dirt track on the same side of the road just a hundred metres ahead. She started to slow down and when she was down to twenty kilometres an hour, she eased her car across the gravel verge. She stopped the car, turned off the ignition and shut off all the lights. She sat nervously in her car on the far edge of the road, in the darkness, waiting for the road train to pass. She could feel beads of perspiration racing down her face. She looked at her mobile phone beside her on the passenger seat. If this didn't work, her next plan was to call her husband, as much as she didn't really want to.

A few seconds later, the giant rig thundered past, raising a cloud of dust and a couple of small stones flipped up against her windscreen. She held her breath as she saw it continue at high speed down the road, its enormous taillights disappearing around the bend ahead.

Bette pushed her full weight back into the driver's seat and stretched her arms back, still clutching the steering wheel tight. She took a few deep breaths, thinking about what to do next. After a couple of quiet minutes, she decided to open her car door and have a quick look and survey the damage done to the rear of her car. She reached for the small flashlight which lived inside her glovebox. She switched it on. But she had to hit it a couple of times before the dim light came on and then she got out.

She walked over the hard, spikey gravel in her high heels shoes and stood at the back of her Holden. She bent down a little. Sure enough, as she shone the flashlight on the bumper, there was a noticeable deep indent just above the number plate.

"Damn idiot bloody driver," she muttered under her breath.

She stretched her body up and started to walk around back to her driver's door. She turned her head when she heard a rumbling sound. It sounded reasonably close. Around the bend ahead, she saw blinding headlights come into view. It sounded like another road train but this time, it was coming fast in the opposite direction. Nothing for her to worry about, being parked on the other side of the road. She lowered her flashlight and grabbed her door handle. As she started to inch the drivers' door open, she was forced to lift her big blue jay eyes for just a fleeting moment.

The headlights seemed to be coming right for her, but she realised that the truck had just turned the bend. She looked away, believing she was quite safe. She stood right back against her car, but the truck had swayed across the broken lines in the centre of the road and turned into the lane next to her. She looked up again too late. The high beams blinded her when she finally did. She raised her arms over her face in defence. Before she could take any more evasive action, the enormous front wide fender brushed her upraised arms, pushing her along the side of her car and the force of the impact snapped her neck in two. She fell dead instantly onto the gravel verge, her body left battered, broken and bleeding behind her car.

Damage done, the rig angled back onto the right side of the road and very rapidly disappeared into the distance and what was left behind it, was blanketed in darkness. It was a cloudy, moonless night.

Minutes ticked by before another vehicle appeared and stopped soon after noticing Bette's parked car. They discovered her mangled body on the road verge and immediately called the emergency number.

Chapter Eight

Raquel was woken by very persistent and loud knocking at the front door of her house. She had fallen asleep on the lounge. She sat up in the half light of her lounge room and had to think for a moment where she actually was. And more importantly, which way to her front door. It had been a long time since she had been in her own home.

She had finally summoned up the courage to walk out on Phil Proctor the other day which had been easier than she had thought. His grouchy and foul-mouthed father Will had helped her make the final decision to leave easy. Will's attitude was the last straw. He had accused her of being a gold-digger because of their age gap and rather than argue with him, she had picked up her handbag and walked out with an armful of clothes to her car and drove away. Proctor tried to call her after she had left, but she switched off her mobile phone straight away.

She had fallen asleep watching an old black and white horror movie on the television. She shot up and glanced up at the clock above the television. It said it was just after five in the morning. She wondered if it was Phil Proctor trying to woo her back. She looked for her slippers but couldn't find them in the dimly lit room. She yawned and stretched her right arm up over her head and walked bare foot through her loungeroom. She opened the latched front door hesitantly and only by an inch to see who was out there.

She saw half the face of Phil Duncan blinking back at her. His brilliant blue eyes behind his glasses were heavy, hooded and red tinged. She unlatched it and opened the door wide. He was standing there, clenching his fists at his sides, his clothes soaking wet from the warm summer rain. His white shirt clung against his chest which made her think what great shape he was in.

"Phil," she gasped, "Are you okay? Is something wrong?"

"Sorry. I'm sorry for coming at this time. It's about Bette," he said, his normally strong, deep voice very serious sounding. He was choking back tears,

"She's dead. Killed."

"Wh-what." She swung the screen door wide open, "What did you just say? Say that again?"

She could now see that his vivid blue eyes were red from tears, "Raquel, I said Bette's dead. My Bette, she's dead. She's really gone."

Raquel took a sharp intake of breath, "What on earth? She can't be. I just saw her earlier tonight. What happened? How could…she be dead? Yeah, I saw her tonight at the pub."

Duncan put his head in his hands and had difficulty holding back a stream of tears, "Oh Christ. It was so terrible. I had to go and identify her body in the morgue. Hardest thing I have ever…had to do, in my life. Can you imagine?"

"What happened, Phil?"

He wiped tears away and tried to regain his composure. Finally, he found the words to continue.

"I am not sure how it happened. They said to me that she

was hit by a semi-trailer on the highway. I don't understand how it happened. I-I loved her, Raquel. Suddenly, she's gone. How can that be real?"

Raquel had never seen Duncan so vulnerable or upset. He was always in control and calm. She reached out for his hand and gently pulled him inside. He was still upset as she put her arms around him and held his wet body close to hers. She hugged him tight against her and the tears started to flow down her cheeks as well. His body was shivering in her arms.

"I know. I know. I loved her too," she said quietly, taking his hand firmly in hers and leading him through her house, around the corridor full of unpacked boxes. His hand felt cold.

"Sit down, right here."

She steered him to the couch in the family room and helped him sit down. He sat on the edge of it. She pushed his shoulders gently back. She sat down next to him and rested her head against his left shoulder. It was a natural gesture, not something she even thought twice about. They sat quietly for a long time, just happy to be in each other's company, thinking about Bette together.

After a while, he carefully lifted her head up from his shoulder and said, "I'd better go now. I shouldn't have come here so late, but I had to tell you. I feel lost. Kind of numb. I'm sorry I've come over so late to tell you."

"It's okay. When did it happen, Phil?"

He shook his head and took a deep breath.

"About nine o'clock they believe. Police wanted to interview me. Still want to interview me some more. Christ. Can you believe they are thinking I am responsible for her…death. There. I have finally said it. I'm, like, their main suspect."

Raquel wiped away more tears, "You're joking. How could they think that way? You're a Detective."

Duncan grunted, "Well, we weren't exactly getting along, her and I. I have to face the facts, Raquel. I pushed her away. I hurt her so much."

She rubbed his arm, "No, no. Don't think like that. Bette always marched to her own tune."

"She went on the Bali honeymoon without me. Bette was angry with me. I also found out that she was talking to another guy she'd met over there. Look. We both were not angels, I guess."

He took a deep breath and then continued, "But I married her because I loved her very, very much. I felt a strong connection with her. I would not go out of my way to hurt her, but I was called upon to do my job. I regret that it upset her that much, that she lost all interest in our marriage. And her faith in me."

She shook her head and touched his shoulder, "No Phil. Don't think negatively about it. You both went separate ways for a moment there, but you would've eventually got back together. I knew that. It was just a matter of time. Time was all you both needed to get past the hurt."

He tried to get up to go but she grabbed his hand and held it tight. This time, his hand was warm, and she couldn't deny that she still felt excitement with his touch.

Duncan looked at her analytically through his swollen red eyes, "I've lost her forever. A second chance now is off the table. I can't get her back. How do you think I feel? I screwed everything up and she never deserved to feel so bad. It's all my fault and I know it."

"Phil, please don't go."

He studied her more closely, "Did you know? I even had an affair while she was away. Did she tell you? See? I'm a complete bastard."

"Phil don't beat yourself up. I'll make us some coffee. And look. You can stay in my spare room tonight."

"I don't want to upset your Proctor."

She shook her head, "It's okay. He's not around at the moment. Under the circumstances, he would understand anyway. The spare room is the last room on the right. The bed is already made up."

"Look. I shouldn't stay here. I am not worth your trouble," he said, wiping his red tinged eyes under his glasses.

Raquel shook her head, "No, I insist. You can't drive home in this sorry state. Just for tonight."

"I was so mean to my wife. A complete bastard," he tried to protest more. but she gently pulled him towards the direction of the spare room.

"It's okay, really. I'll just go get you a towel and a glass of cold water."

He sat down on the edge of the bed reluctantly, his head bowed.

"You know the police think it was me. I know how it goes. Our first suspect is always the one who is the closest to the victim. I am no different. But I truly loved Bette."

She disappeared into her kitchen, then to the laundry to grab a clean bath towel. By the time she entered the spare room, with glass and towel in hand, she found Duncan lying on the top of the bed, already sound asleep. She realised he must have been exhausted. She quietly placed the glass of water and towel on the tallboy and grabbed a throw from the velvet armchair in the corner. She carefully placed it over his sleeping body. He was still dressed in his wet clothes, but she felt his forehead to check his temperature.

"You're fine," she whispered softly near his ear, "And you're safe here."

Raquel thought he looked like a sleeping little boy. He was lying on his left side, spread eagled across the double bed. She leaned over him again and removed his eyeglasses and placed them carefully on the bedside table next to him. She retreated from the spare room.

She shut the bedroom door as quietly as she could and padded bare foot into her kitchen. She switched on a tall standard lamp rather than the main fluoro light and made herself an instant coffee. She sat on a stool, shed some tears for her best friend and wondered what to say to Duncan in the morning. It felt strange to have Phil Duncan under her own roof again. Even just for one innocent night.

****

She finally opened her red tinged eyes to the sound of magpies singing high in the trees and to strong sunlight streaming through her bedroom window. She had slept in past her alarm, so she leapt out of bed, rubbed her eyes and threw her T-shirt over her head and struggled into a pair of jeans. She forgot her bra.

It was a manoeuvre well planned as her mobile started to ring, accompanied by pounding noises on her front door. She rubbed the sleep out of her eyes and realised that her son was calling.

"Are you seriously knocking at my door?" she answered the phone brightly, brushing and patting her tangled bed hair back into some order.

"Yeah. I left my house key at Nan's."

"Okay, okay. Hold your horses. I'm on my way."

She closed the call. She opened the door, wrapping an arm subconsciously across her chest as her policeman son slipped inside the house, looking casual in his black long sleeve T-shirt and jeans. He was clearly off duty.

"Raquel, I'm actually looking for Detective Duncan. I saw his car parked outside in the street. But I can't locate him. He's not even answering his mobile."

"Is that really why you're here? You're looking for him?"

He stood in the lounge room, plunging his hands into his jean pockets and looking strangely serious, "No, well. I had some bad news too. I think you should sit down."

Raquel sighed heavily, "I think I know, honey. It's about Bette Duncan. I already know she's dead."

Steve raised an eyebrow in surprise and said, "News travels fast in Brumby Flat. I' m sorry. I know you were best friends. But how did you find out?"

"That, she's dead? Her husband came to see me last night."

Steve was quiet for a moment, thinking hard about what she had just said.

"What? Detective Duncan is here? He stayed the night? Here? With you? Alone?" he exclaimed.

"Look, It's not like that. Please. Keep your voice down. He's still asleep."

"Oh, wow. The town's going to implode with this information. His wife's dead and he's run straight back into your arms. I can't believe it," Steve threw his hands up in the air, then he turned around wildly, "No, actually, I do believe it. You two had this thing going for a while, before you hooked up with old Tex. I remember now."

"No, No. He's in the spare room asleep. Nothing is happening between the two of us. He looked awful last night, so I put him up in the spare room. And keep your voice down. He's probably still sound asleep."

She touched her forefinger to her lips, but Steve kept talking excitedly.

"I reckon you should wake him up. You know, it's probably not a good idea to be protecting him. I can't go into…police business with you."

"He's under suspicion, isn't he? Yes, I know all about that too."

"No. Don't tell me anymore. I think you should stay out of it. Get him up and get him out of here. Do me a favour and keep well away from Detective Duncan for now. Promise me?"

Raquel glared back at her son, one hand on hip, "I can't promise you anything like that. But I can promise you that I'll do what Bette would want me to do."

He shook his head and snorted, "She would not endorse you bedding her husband."

"Well, he's not asleep in *my* bedroom. We're not involved," she snapped back, "That's not a nice thing to say to your mother. Don't judge me so harshly. Go and have a look at yourself, if you must look the fool."

"Okay. Okay. I believe you. But get him out of here as soon as possible. Crap. I have to go."

She reached out and grabbed his arm, "Can you tell me what happened to her?"

He looked down at his feet, "I'm sorry but I can't really

discuss it. I hope you understand. But it's going to be in all the papers and social media by tomorrow. Sure to be."

Raquel arched an eyebrow and let him go. He crossed the room in one long stride and closed the front door soundly behind him.

She crossed her arms, fuming in silence and stood there in the centre of her lounge room for a while. She had now started to wish she hadn't allowed Duncan to stay the night. The idea of it had certainly made her policeman son nearly go over the edge.

She heard a noise behind her and turned to find Duncan dressed in the same clothes which were now completely dry. He stood there, wiping his eyeglasses with a small cloth.

"I thought I heard voices," he said in his strong, rich tone which had returned.

"Hey. You're up. It was just my son. He was checking up on me."

"Did he say much to you?"

"Oh no. I don't want to play this game," she replied, raising her hands in the air. "I am not going to be in the middle of this with you two."

"What do you mean?"

"Go home, Detective Phillip Duncan. I need to be on my own. Okay? I can't make it plainer than that, can I?"

She saw the hurt and confused look play out in his intensely attractive blue eyes. But he did exactly what she asked of him. He did not argue. Without saying another word, he left her side and simply walked out.

Chapter Nine

For the next two days, the town of Brumby Flat was grand gossip central. Raquel had read the local papers, watched the news and explored the internet. Everywhere she turned, someone had an opinion on Mrs. Bette Duncan's tragic and untimely death. Overwhelmingly, accusing eyes, finger pointing, and suspicion fell on her new husband.

She was seated at her dining table, pouring over the latest news report. The journalists were not very kind. They painted Phil Duncan into the worst kind of monster, a neglectful husband. The fact that two years ago, Detective Duncan had stopped the Brumby Flat serial killer was brushed over and long forgotten so it seemed. There were eyewitness accounts of the wedding reception and the fact that Bette honeymooned on her own in Bali did not go unnoticed. The journos had done their research thoroughly and dished up every juicy titbit they could find.

She now knew every gruesome aspect of Bette's death. The press tried to convince their readers that she was not killed by accident. Her husband was under suspicion and had sufficient motive to order her murder. Raquel started to cry again. She threw the newspaper down in disgust. She had read about enough. She was sure it was all lies, designed to sell newspapers. She knew Duncan had truly loved her best friend. One headline screamed 'Murder town reawakens: Suspect Detective hubby walks free'.

She walked out into the main street, not knowing where she was heading. She just needed to walk and clear her head.

"Hey. Raquel. Raquel. Wait."

She spun right around in the main street, when she heard her name being called out. It was Detective Duncan who came running up to her. He was wearing his best pinstripe shirt and tan trousers.

"I didn't get the chance to say thank you the other day. Thanks for supporting me through all this madness. I am in the media every day unfortunately."

She smiled and nodded, suddenly feeling a bit shy knowing that all eyes would be on them right now. "It's okay. I don't need your thanks, honestly I don't."

"I'm sorry if I pushed you a bit hard…Wait. Can we have a coffee at…" he stopped in midsentence, remembering that the Raindrops Shop was now closed. It had been Bette's enterprise, another part of her life he had to eventually deal with. At this moment of time, Kitty Caulfield who was still lying in a coma and Bette's tragic death were all consuming him.

He shook his head and averted his eyes from her.

She took a step forward and said, "Yes sure, we can. I have the keys to the Raindrops Shop. I also think Bette would like me to keep the shop open. I wanted to have a chat to you about that."

Raquel's heart was moved. She crossed the street in three quick strides and pulled him into her arms. She hugged him tight and with some reluctance, he physically surrendered to her warm embrace and gently rested his hands on her hips. He buried his face into her right shoulder. He wanted to cry but he knew he had no tears left.

Her heart was pounding like mad inside her chest and she secretly hoped Duncan was oblivious to its' increased rhythm. It was so wrong to harbour these strong feelings for him still. She thought she was well over him a long time ago.

As luck would have it, Phil Proctor had just left the new Post Office further across and down the street with a bundle of US mail in his hands. He was grinning broadly until he saw Raquel Willaston and Detective Duncan locked in an embrace in the middle of the empty main street. He stopped his confident swagger, took a sharp intake of breath and shoved the mail into his back pocket. He bent his head, then removed his Akubra hat and punched the inside of it with his right fist. He turned his back on them and drifted away, deep into the shadows of a shop veranda. He decided to walk home to his cottage through the back streets.

Finally, they let go of each other. Duncan stood back and probed her face with his intense stare. She realised that he finally knew the truth.

"You're supposed to hate me."

"When you are not so charming, I usually do."

She looked down, suddenly feeling awkward.

He leaned in so close that she could feel his hot breath on her right cheek.

"I can't do this right now," he whispered to her, gently taking and curling a wispy strand of her hair over her left shoulder, "I've just lost my wife, you know that. I can't entertain these sorts of thoughts, just now. Do you understand me?"

Raquel nodded, daring not to raise her eyes to look into his, "Of course I do. I am sorry if I am giving you the wrong impression."

He smirked and added, "However, I know I'm an irresistible cad."

"Now you're taking it bloody too far. But that you are."

He leant in again, keeping his voice low, "I'll catch up one day soon, just to talk, but I have to see if I can find out what happened to Bette. Was it an accident? I just don't know."

She nodded and turned to walk away and as she did, she recognised trouble coming in their direction. It was a threat Duncan was not yet aware of. She only knew as she recognised a couple of the faces from two years earlier.

"Phil, the journos are here. You might want to disappear now."

"Oh shit!" he exclaimed. He walked off swiftly with the press in hot pursuit. She headed straight home. She wasn't followed. Fortunately, they had missed seeing their embrace.

****

Constable Steve Willaston had experienced a day and a half rolled into one. He had spent most of his twelve-hour shift dealing with a minor car accident on the highway, directing traffic in the main street for the town's resident mother duck and her ten ducklings and then he had to fill in for the lollipop man at the high school crossing. The lollipop man had a severe bout of flu and a bad case of the runs.

Then, at the last minute, Steve had to interview another wedding guest because head office had advised that Senior Detective Phillip Duncan was definitely off the case. But he figured that would be right due to all the recent media coverage on Bette Duncan's tragic death which was still under intense investigation.

Steve had just finished his long shift, when his mobile suddenly rang. He looked at the screen before he answered, genuinely surprised to find it was Yankee Tanaka. She had never called him before. He hadn't seen her for the last two weeks, since he had dropped by their home.

"Hello, Constable Willaston here."

She sighed heavily on the other end and then spoke in her accent strangely peppered with a mix of American, Estonian and Japanese overtones.

"I know it's you. I was wondering if you had some time for me tonight."

"What did you have in mind, Kristina?"

"What we talked about. The last time."

"Oh. Okay. Well, do we discuss it over dinner at the pub?"

"Oh fuck no. We don't."

"We could go for a drive then," he suggested.

"So pick me up, Mr. Policeman. Soon as you can."

The phone call ended abruptly in his ear.

He stood there smiling for a long minute. He quickly raced home and noticed that his mother wasn't around. He removed his police uniform and put on a long sleeve black T-shirt and his best dark jeans. He nearly forgot the most important item. At the last second, he picked up the police issue handcuffs and stuffed them in his jeans side pocket. He saw the yellow Pontiac parked in the side garage and grabbed the spare keys. Obviously, Raquel wasn't in need of her car just at the moment. It was the perfect ride for his night of adventure.

He drove with some excitement to the Tanaka residence. He roared to a stop at the front of their house and he quickly realised that she must have been excited as well. Yankee Tanaka shot straight out through the front door, earbuds in her ears and with her mobile in hand. She looked amazing as always, dressed simply in a plain white crop top and a pair of navy track pants. She jumped into the passenger seat next to him, and briefly looked at him, mesmerising him with her wide almond eyes. Her long brown hair brushed her thighs, and he could smell lavender bath salts.

"Where are you taking me?" she asked.

"There's a scenic lookout. It's not too far away."

"Will we be alone?"

"That's the plan. Your parents know you're with me, right?"

"Oh yeah," she made a face he couldn't read.

Topham Hill was the town's own version of inspiration point. It was just two kilometres down the highway, on the first left. He drove up the hilly road, which was mostly bitumen, then turned to gravel.

When Steve parked, he noticed there was another car parked further up. A white station wagon. He turned the ignition off and the car interior went dark. There was a clear sky that evening with light beaming from the full moon and the twinkling blanket of stars above.

They adjusted their seats a little further back.

Yankee was the first to break the awkward silence.

"Well, Mr. Policeman. Did you bring the cuffs with you?"

He smirked at her, "How could I forget them. I'll show you later. Why don't we talk? You first?"

"I'm not your kind of girl. You know all about me from

my parents. They want me to go to that big space agency you know. I don't even like you."

Her eyes flicked to her mobile phone and she sent a text message to someone somewhere as she spoke to him.

Steve didn't know how to react to her frank admission. He wasn't so much upset by it, except just perplexed. She was unusually cold and distant. He was starting to wonder if he would be able to break down her icy composure at all.

"Okay so what are we going to talk about?"

She shrugged her shoulders and stated, "Show us the cuffs."

He reluctantly took them out of his pocket and her almond eyes lit up as big as saucers.

"Police issue, are they?"

"Yes."

"Go on. Put them on me, Mr. Policeman. Do it."

"I can't do that."

"What's your problem," she reached across and grabbed them from his hands and before he had time to react, she had fastened one cuff to her wrist and snapped the other around his left wrist.

Steve slapped his forehead, wrenching her cuffed arm forward, "Why did you do that? I was trying to tell you... I left the keys back at the station. Now what am I going to do about this situation?" he exclaimed.

She studied him through whisps of hair, "Relax. Do me here in the car."

Steve's mind started to race, not to mention his heart rate had increased. As much as he desired her, he wasn't expecting to hear these words issue from her lips. He had convinced himself that she was still an innocent schoolgirl.

"Are you serious? Yankee. We have to somehow drive down the hill and get the fucking keys. You're going to have to cooperate with me on this."

"No." she snapped back. Then she leaned her chest forward, her nipples like hard raisons brushing his left arm. As he discovered then, she wasn't wearing a bra. Her bee sting lips pressed eagerly against his. She planted a big sloppy, inexperienced kiss on him which he then tried to control, but she was forceful. He realised that his anticipation and expectations of their first intimacy were not going to be met. He was disappointed and now realised she was far too young for him. He pushed her away and wiped his lips dry with his free right hand. She opened her large almond eyes, her lips still moist and glared at him.

"I am serious. We have to go back to the station now, Yankee."

"No," she snapped.

She pulled herself towards the passenger door. The handcuffs drawing tight against their wrists. Steve pulled her hard the opposite way and accidentally leaned against the door handle.

Suddenly, the drivers' door swung wide open and they both half fell out of the car. He was on his back with Yankee's pretty oval face looking up, her long brown hair half covering Steve's surprised face.

"Constable Willaston," Duncan was standing over them, looking quite shocked himself. Behind him, Steve saw his mother craning her neck to see what was happening.

"What are you doing up here?"

"We are testing his handcuffs, and they work okay," Yankee replied but not too convincing.

"Oh, are you just?" he smirked, his eyes twinkling behind his glasses.

"And why are you up here, Detective Duncan? Parking? And with my mother?" Steve remarked.

Duncan suddenly averted his eyes, "You got me there, only we were just talking. We are completely innocent."

"Yes, well, so are we."

"Righto. I'll leave you both to it then."

Duncan turned to Raquel but stopped when Steve yelled out, "Wait. Wait a minute."

"What?"

"I don't have the keys…for these."

He rattled the handcuffs on his wrist and Yankee's.

Duncan started to laugh heartily while Raquel behind him was biting her lip trying not to react. Duncan finally removed his glasses and rubbed away the tears of laughter in his eyes, "Okay son. Well. This is your lucky night. I have a spare set in my car consol. I'll go get them. And go home, the pair of you," he wagged his finger at Steve, "No more undercover police work tonight."

He found them and tossed the handcuff keys effortlessly to Steve. Taking his advice, Steve started the Pontiac and drove off, down the hill.

Duncan returned to his parked car. Raquel was back inside it, rubbing her bare arms. He climbed back into the driver's seat and noticed her shivering.

"Are you cold?"

"Just a little."

"Here," he leaned over and grabbed his brown check jacket from the back seat, "Put this over your shoulders. You know. Your son was funny tonight. He's not a bad kid, but I don't know about the company he's keeping at the moment."

Raquel nodded, "That Tanaka girl. Yeah, I think she's trouble but I think the crush will pass. That's what it is. Thankfully, it's just a crush. She's a bit too young for my son."

"Sorry we had to meet up here. I feel eyes watching the house all the time. And as I was saying before the interruption, I'm off the case now. Not happy but can't do anything about it."

He rolled down his drivers' side window and placed his elbow over it.

"That's rough. It's okay, Phil. I get it. I just hope my Phil Proctor is not out looking for me."

"I thought you would tell him you were meeting me."

She bit her bottom lip, "I was going to, I had planned to, but I think…look, it doesn't really matter. He doesn't care what I do now. I think we grew apart a while ago."

He took his glasses off, wiped them on his shirt and said philosophically,

"Well. There was a bit of an age gap between you two. I think that in itself can be hard work."

She gave him a lopsided smile, "It's only hard work when every bloody woman in town practically throws themselves at him. Because he's this easy-going American cowboy."

"And a man of the world," he added, "A talented one at that. The silos look bloody amazing. I have to admit his silo art does bring people to town."

"Yeah. That it does."

He took a deep breath and added, "Although I am curious about the last silo project in the region. I didn't know we had a bushranger element near here, but he did a good job capturing that image. But the guy on the horse looked more pony express than Aussie bushranger."

She shrugged her shoulders and replied in his defence, "It's called artistic licence."

"Now, on a more serious subject," she said, half turning her body around in the passenger seat, "Did you have any ideas on suspects?"

"For our coma girl, yes I did. I was working from a list, but I can't follow it up now."

"Why not?"

"It's not my case anymore. I did leave case notes with my colleague. Hopefully, things will get followed up. Don't know."

There was a long silence. But it wasn't an uncomfortable one. It was a retrospective and mutually respectful one.

Eventually, she sighed heavily and Duncan swiftly turned his penetrating blue eyes to study her closely and intensely.

"You believe I wouldn't have harmed her? Right?"

She hesitated before offering him her answer.

"You hurt her; I know. She talked about it. But you're not a killer, Phil."

"How do you truly know? What if...I really wanted to be with you? How would I get inside your head or be with you, while my Bette's alive and breathing?"

She looked at him, her hazel eyes wide. Then she relaxed and smiled back when she saw the mischievous glint in his eye.

"I don't believe it for a minute. It's not funny at all."

He smirked, "Yes, you're right. Just testing you. I'm not as crazy as the papers would have you believe. But I have to say this. Whether it's right or wrong, I still like you. You're blunt and honest about everything."

"I can't see anything wrong with that. You did tell my son we were innocently talking. And yes, we are."

He nodded. He then looked out the car window, thinking about their conversation. He thought about his suspect list and realised he had to somehow ensure the investigations he had started were continued. It required a plan of action.

"Well, I think we'll wrap it up tonight. Thanks for listening. I'll drop you back in town, okay."

Chapter Ten

Proctor called her while she was still at the winery, dealing with a major IT issue. The office girl had accidentally changed internet providers while she was redoing her eye makeup and the new system wasn't working or connecting. Raquel had already spent two hours on the phone trying to disconnect to reconnect to the correct service provider.

Proctor had asked her over to the cottage for a home cooked meal. Right away, she was suspicious about his offer of dinner. She had an idea that the news was not very good for her.

She didn't wish to go, but she had to know what he was up to. They had not talked for more than a week. She finally arrived at her home at six o'clock and quickly changed into her favourite cotton floral dress. She touched up her eye makeup in the bathroom mirror and noticed how tired she looked from the frustrations of her workday.

She drove up the hill to the cottage and knocked on the front door. She still had the spare front door key in her handbag but out of respect, she declined to use it to let herself in. She didn't want to upset him.

From within, she heard his cowboy boots echo in the long hallway. Proctor opened the door wide and leaned against the door frame, looking resplendent in his checked Western shirt and best tight jeans. He ran his other hand through his mane of grey hair and smiled at her, his eyes obviously admiring her frame unashamedly.

"Hey girlie. Great to see you again," he moved to one side, to allow her to pass. "Come in. I made us a real Texas barbeque."

She peered around the door and secretly wished she could see through walls.

He noticed her hesitation.

"What's wrong, girlie?"

"Is your father Will around?"

He shook his head, "Nope. He's at the ranch next door if you like. Won't be back until morning, I reckon. He talks a lot with them. We will be alone, sweetheart."

"I have to admit, I am not very hungry tonight," she told him as she settled into a chair in the dining room. She could see that he had gone to a lot of trouble, laying down a lace tablecloth and setting the table. He had even placed a white pillar candle on a small plate as the table centrepiece. He lit it carefully with a match.

"I don't want to waste good food. Just eat what you can," he brought out a plate of sausages and rump steak and placed it right under her nose. He had put down a glass of champagne on her right.

He sat down opposite her with his own plate of food and cracked open a can of beer, "Hope, you like it. My old man, he taught me how to Texas barbeque."

She picked up her knife and folk and cut a small piece of steak. She chewed it slowly and nodded, "Wow. Really good. Nicely smoked."

They were quiet for a few minutes, enjoying the dinner.

"Now girlie. I'm sure glad you came over tonight. We need to thrash things out."

She quickly interrupted him, "Just say what's on your mind, Phil. I've had a busy day."

He looked down at his hands on the table, "My darling girl, it's time for me to say my goodbyes. It's been a crazy, wild rollercoaster ride with you. But now it's time for me to travel around a bit. Going to Sydney first and then we'll be returning to my New York city."

She nodded, "Okay."

"I would stay longer here but my money's going to run out. I have to look for a new project to do. And pretty soon too."

Raquel cut another piece, had a bite and said nothing.

"Yes ma'am. Don't expect me to come back either. I will always remember you, you're here in my heart and soul. But I won't be coming back for you. We're finished, girlie. You knew it was coming anyway. We lost that tight connection we had, but we've had some fine times together, hey?"

"Wow, that's some kind of break up speech. Thank you very much."

She swallowed hard, holding back tears which pricked away at her eyelashes and she got up to leave. She placed the cutlery she had used in the centre of her plate.

"What are you doing?" he rose to his feet.

"Phil, I have to go. I am not a fan of goodbyes. And by the way, I was never your bloody possession to push around your own chessboard or something. I thought I meant something to you, after the picnic you made me think…"

He leapt around the dining table and spun her around by

her shoulders. He pressed her against him with his strong arms. She tried to wrestle out of his grasp, but he held her tight to his chest. She could feel he was aroused but she was determined to do her best and resist his affections.

"You've misunderstood me. Do you really think you meant nothing to me?" he growled in his low whisper of a voice, "I loved you, girlie, and I do still love you. But things change sometimes, and we are powerless to fight against it. I am genuinely sorry about that, ma'am."

"Please. Let me go, Phil," she snapped.

"Before we go our separate ways, we should kiss goodbye…at least for old time's sake…"

She managed to push him away, "No. Definitely not. You've made your decision. So, have I. I will move on too. Goodbye Phil Proctor. I won't come looking for you either."

She brushed past him and headed to the front door, with Proctor in hot pursuit.

"Hey. I saw your catch up with the detective in the street. It looked kind of real cosy to me. I figure that's who you prefer spending your time with nowadays."

She turned on her heel and stood frowning at him, "And what's that supposed to mean *exactly*?"

He shrugged his broad shoulders, hands thrust in his jeans side pockets, "Just saying looks like you'd rather hug him than me. He's just lost his wife, for God's sake."

"Okay. I have to spell it out. That poor guy is very upset because he's just lost his wife, who was my best friend. He needs someone in town to believe in him. There's nothing sordid going on. You're acting all crazy over nothing. I thought you would understand his pain better than anyone else in town. And understand my damn pain as well. How dare you, Phil? How bloody dare you?"

She shoved her way past him as the tears came rushing down her cheeks.

"Wait my sweetheart. I am sorry. I didn't mean to say that. I'm an idiot. Don't end this badly. We had a lot of fine times, you know."

As she prepared to walk out, Will Proctor stumbled through the front door and tipped his shabby old fishing hat at her.

"Get out of my way, you miserable old goat," she said coolly under her breath.

Will leaned forward, his right ear cupped by his hand and his crinkled blue eyes frowning, "What did you say?"

"I said I'm on my way out to get my old coat," she snapped at him loudly.

Her final answer was the slamming of the front door in both their faces.

Phil Proctor stood there in the hallway, hands resting on hips. Will shrugged his shoulders and made haste in the direction of the bathroom. Proctor sighed and swept his hand over his silver grey hair. He was left alone with his own thoughts. He knew that would be the last time he would see Raquel Willaston. He realised that he could have handled their last moments together much better, but it was too late to fix it.

The suitcases were already packed. Proctor and his father Will were ready to leave in two days' time, as planned.

****

Just an hour before, Raquel had heard the fire siren go off

in the township. She had her bushfire plan ready to go if needed. However, she was at Proctor's borrowed cottage that day, tying up some loose ends.

Raquel had grabbed her Akubra hat from the hat rack by the kitchen back door, walked outside and lifted her head to the sky. She could see the thick plumes of smoke far on the horizon, but she instinctively knew the fire was moving quite rapidly in the direction of Brumby Flat. There was a dry southerly wind fanning the flames. She had never faced a bushfire threat before, but being a hot, windy day, she assumed there was just a small window of time to prepare and leave. Instinctively, she knew that it was time to leave immediately.

Proctor had left Brumby Flat the day before, finally off to explore the rest of the country and he had left the black mare behind in the stables. She had planned to return the mare to the McCarthys the next day. She didn't foresee this bushfire danger looming, but it was good timing in a sense. If the cottage went up in flames, it wouldn't really matter if she had cleaned it or not.

With her dog Maxine nervously scampering around her heels, Raquel was preparing to saddle up the mare and ride her out of danger. She didn't know what to do with her Pontiac Firebird but she had the car fully insured and if it was damaged by fire, so be it. She knew she had to leave right now.

The mare was tossing and shaking her glossy black head and mane restlessly, as she fiddled with the buckles under her belly. Finally saddled up, Raquel had another battle with the bridle. Finally, the black mare took the bit. She had started to lead the black mare out of the stables when she saw a police car drive up fast. It was her policeman son who jumped out and ran up to her.

"You're leaving, oh good. It's really bad over the hills. Burning out of control. I've been talking to the Firies on the ground."

"Steve, honey, I was checking social media just before and there's a few locals staying on the edge of town, they're going to try and defend their homes, they said. I saved our valuable stuff and photos, it's all in the cellar at our house. In case the fire gets too close."

"What? Oh fuck, really? Who's staying behind?"

"Your Yankee friend and I think Anabella is too,"

Steve's heart skipped a beat, "Christ. I need to take your car. Now."

"Honey. It's been acting up…"

"I need a fast car, Raquel. Please. And where are you going?"

"I have to save the mare. I'll ride her up to the McCarthy's property. And stay there. At least they are out a bit further. I'll be perfectly safe."

Steve put his right palm out.

She reluctantly felt in the back pocket of her jeans, nodded her head and threw him the car key.

"Please. Please. Just be careful. Don't put your own life at risk for them or anyone else. And what about your police car?"

Steve yelled back to her, "I'll come back for it, if I can. I'll be okay. Just leave now. I love you."

"Love you too. Stay safe."

He turned around again and said, "I'm sorry about Bette. I liked her."

"Thanks honey. I didn't see Bette's going…coming. You know?"

He ran to the Pontiac and clicked the ignition over quickly. There was no time to waste. Raquel watched her son speed down the dirt road and took a deep breath. Under it, she said very quietly, "Keep safe, son."

She shook her flyaway hair back and firmly placed her Akubra on her head. She swung up into the saddle and gently tapped her heels into the belly of the black mare to propel her forward. At a steady trot, they headed towards the dirt road and she dearly hoped to safety. Maxine followed behind the mare at a brisk run, but she stopped and crouched nervously at times.

****

In the distance, the sky over Brumby Flat was glowing a brilliant orange red. Huge plumes of thick black and grey smoke could be seen rising high above the treetops. A couple of planes were circling and swooping with fire retardant.

Steve pulled up in the Pontiac in front of the Tanaka residence and jumped out. Small embers and ash were falling all around him. A high wall of flames could be seen just past a canopy of trees in the distance.

Yankee was standing in the middle of their front yard, wearing her best ripped hipster jeans and a sloppy black T-shirt. She was coughing madly, holding up a long sleeve to cover her nose and mouth. With her other hand, she was spraying the roof of the family home randomly with a plain garden hose.

Steve came up behind her and calmly grabbed her right

arm. She slightly turned her head and a tiny glimmer in her eye suggested she was secretly pleased to see him. She let the garden hose go, failing across the ground, like an angry snake.

Steve talked directly into her left ear, "I am here to get you out."

She shook her head and glared at him, "I can't just go. This is my home."

"Yankee, the house is nothing. Possessions are nothing. That is a goddamn firestorm coming over the hill. You can't win this battle. No one can win against what's coming this way."

He reached out and grabbed her left hand.

She started to scream at him and tried to wrestle out of his firm grasp, "But it's our home. Everything we have is in there. I need to save our home."

"Where's your family?"

"They went to the city, shopping. I have to stay here and try to save our home. It's been left to me to do it."

"No. You need to listen to me, Yankee. You are someone special to me and I can't replace you. Your family would never forgive me if I left you here. We have to leave now, before it's too late. Let the house burn to the ground. It's time to go. We have to leave, right now, before we can't make it out."

"But I have to stay.," she started to protest again.

He cut her off in midsentence and gently but firmly pulled her towards the car, "Stop. No more buts. It's time to go. Don't argue with me. I had to practically steal my mother's sportscar to get you out."

"I'll just get our photo albums, okay? I know where my mom keeps them. And what about the old lady on the corner?

You have to take her too."

"Anabella Williams? She's here too? Quick. You have two minutes. That's it."

Kristina did as she was told. She returned to the car and quickly dumped an armload of precious family photo albums into the back seat of the car. Steve put his foot down on the accelerator hard and roared up to the front of Anabella's house. He honked the car horn furiously until Anabella made her appearance, peering nervously out.

"Hey, we have to leave now. You can't stay here. The fire's changed direction," he yelled out to her through cupped hands.

Anabella walked onto her porch, elegantly dressed in a purple shift dress, white ankle boots and a teased hairdo. Her eyes showed her stress. She bent over and pulled out a suitcase from the hallway. Steve waved her over and she attempted to drag the suitcase towards the car. She had trouble dragging it. He realised the heavy suitcase was going to slow them down, so he put the car handbrake on and climbed out. He grabbed the heavy suitcase from her and lifted it effortlessly into the boot.

"Sorry. You'll have to climb through into the back seat," he explained, flicking the drivers' seat down for her.

"I don't think I should go. It's our home," she said, looking at him through her false eyelashes, "I am sure the fire trucks are coming soon. They'll save all the houses here."

Steve put his hands on his hips and raised his voice to one of authority.

"No Anabella. We are all going together. This fire is way too close."

She reluctantly ducked her head and dived into the back

seat. Steve turned the ignition on again.

"Okay, hold on everyone. We'll have to put some distance between us and the fire front."

He felt Kristina tug excitedly on his arm, "Oh my god. Look. I think we're cut off on both sides. See the smoke over there."

"Oh shit," he looked up, but had taken his eyes off the dirt road. He lost control of the Pontiac which swung side to side and Anabella screamed behind him. A large kangaroo appeared on the roadside but bounded off back into the bushes unhurt. Steve finally regained control of the car just as a set of headlights loomed ahead in the slight smoky haze. He stopped in time before they collided. The fire truck skidded to a halt on the dirt track and several Firies jumped out. The closest one removed their protective helmet. She let her ash blonde hair brush over the shoulders of her yellow uniform. He noticed at once her expressive pale blue eyes, turned up nose and wide lips. She was half a foot shorter than him and all the other Firies were taller than her too.

"Thank goodness we found you," she said, smiling up at him, a dimple forming in the hollow of her right cheek, "You need to leave."

"That's exactly what we were trying to do."

She put out her slender hand, and he shook it firmly, "I'm Kimberley. You can't go this way. You're better off going north. Then go around left on Cemetery Road, then head right back into town. We'll do what we can here. Is there anyone else left back there, officer?"

Steve shook his head, "I'm not sure. I knew about these two ladies. I'm Constable Steve Willaston by the way."

She raised an eyebrow, "Well, nice to meet you," she

started to put on her work gloves, "Okay guys," she yelled out, turning to her team. She put her helmet back on and pulled down her visor, "We're ahead of the fire. Let's get organised. Sam, you look after young Jim. Move quickly everyone."

She then turned around to Steve and said, "And you, Constable, should be halfway back down that road by now."

He waved his hand at her and reversed the car with the other hand. He put it into gear, but the car stalled. He shook his head, cursed and tried the ignition again. The engine made a spluttering, choking sound but did not turn over.

Kimberley looked over her shoulder and frowned. She trotted up to the drivers' side window and said, "You have to go now."

He turned the key again, but the same noises came from the engine. Anabella was freaking out in the backseat, but Yankee still looked calm, flicking her hair out of her eyes.

"I am trying but I have to be careful, I don't want to flood the bloody engine."

They could all smell the smoke, and it was only a matter of time before flames would be visible in the trees ahead.

He gave it another half minutes' rest and then turned the key. This time, the Firebird's engine burst into life. With a wave of his hand to Kimberley, he pushed the accelerator to the floor.

As they drove back and flew past the Tanaka family home, Kristina finally piped up and gave her opinion on their recent encounter, "She really, really noticed you," she said drily, her arms crossed over her chest. Her long brown hair was sprayed over one shoulder.

Steve held his eyes on the road, but he could feel her

almond eyes glaring at him.

"We both wear uniforms. We both respect authority. We have to uphold the law and keep order, you know."

"I think you know what I'm talking about."

He sighed audibly, "You're overreacting, Yankee. We have our jobs to do. That's it."

But he knew that she had a point. Steve had noticed Kimberley too. She was in charge of the situation, and she looked like she knew what she was doing. He had to admit that he was impressed with how confident she was. He had to admit she was pretty too but not exotically attractive like Yankee Tanaka. He really hoped he would see Kimberley again. He had to learn more about what made her tick.

He was thankful when Yankee took a phone call from her worried parents and the subject of Kimberley was completely dropped.

Chapter Eleven

Steve Willaston did catch up with Kimberley Ann Jackson five hours later, when the fire threat was finally over. Just as the fire raged around the first row of houses on the edge of town, the heavens had opened and unleashed a torrent of rain. Two truckloads of exhausted Firies descended on Brumby Flat for a well-earned reprieve and they were gathered around, downing cold drinks purchased from the service station.

Steve had managed to make it safely back to Proctor's cottage and he drove his police car back into town. Proctor's piece of land was untouched by the fire. Steve had joined police from the next district in sealing off roads during the threat and telling farmers and locals to evacuate their properties. He had received a quick call later from Yankee Tanaka advising that their family home had fortunately survived the fire, but she said it was a close call. She also said her parents were unusually rattled by the entire event.

He called Raquel and she was also okay. The McCarthy's had her join them for a cold meats and salad lunch. It wasn't the type of day to put on a Texas barbeque as Will Proctor had taught them to do.

Constable Steve parked the police car alongside the kerb. He straightened his uniform and confidently walked up to

Kimberley who was drinking a diet lemonade straight from a can. She had removed her visor, she shook her hair free and rubbed her pert nose which was covered in brown smudges. Her pale blue eyes shone bright as she turned to look at him. Her uniform was torn in a couple of places near her right elbow and clearly smoke damaged. His approach did not go unnoticed by the other Firies who smirked, postured and nudged each other.

"Hey there, Constable Steve." She said with a smile and a wink, leaning back against the soiled fire truck, "Pretty full on, wasn't it today?"

He smiled back, "Wow, yeah. That was my first real fire involvement."

"You did really well, Steve. It's not an easy job. It was a bad fire and I thought we'd lost control over it a couple of times. Left us with about sixty hectares of scorched earth."

"How long have you been a Firie?"

She swept the beads of sweat off her brow with her right hand, "I started about five years ago. Joined up straight after my parents died."

"I'm sorry to hear they're gone."

"So am I," she said in a quiet, reflective voice, "My brother and I have been without them for a while. We've learnt to cope."

Kimberley Ann Jackson did not tell him what happened to her parents. Her life had changed quite dramatically seven years ago. Their family farm was just situated a kilometre outside of Brumby Flat. She and her younger brother Darren had enjoyed being raised on the farm surrounded by pigs, chickens and sheep. Their parents were hardworking, but always made sure they shared their children's biggest events.

One summers day, while Kimberley and Darren were away on a school camp, their parents woke up to see a large blazing glow at the base of their bottom paddock. They didn't have much time to pack their Ute with personal effects and drive away. The story was that the bushfire quickly surrounded the farmhouse on all sides due to high northerly winds and the only way out was the winding, gravel driveway. They were caught in the flames as they tried desperately to escape. Kimberley was the first to learn of their fate from her biology teacher.

She immediately dropped out of high school and grief stricken, she got into some unsuitable situations. She started to learn pole dancing but realised very quickly that it did not release her inner rage. She tried firing at targets on a rifle range and once again, she was left feeling empty inside. Then she joined up as a volunteer Firefighter and she raged against fire, her new sworn enemy. It wasn't long before her talent was recognised, and she was elevated to paid cadet. But still, it wasn't enough to take the edge off her inner rage. She tried joining a six-week French pastry class to learn about cooking, a chess group, a local hockey team and even, the local golf club. Nothing was dangerous enough for her. Then she found out about women's boxing. She joined up and whenever she had the chance to go to the city, she would engage in boxing matches.

Reality brought her back to Brumby Flat when Steve said, "I hope you don't mind me saying this. But I'd like to ask you to join me for a meal one day? Can be lunch, dinner, whatever you want."

She laughed, the attractive dimple appearing in the hollow of her right cheek,

"What? Are you asking me out on a date?"

He shrugged his shoulders and suddenly felt shy over it, "Yeah, I guess it's a date of sorts."

"How old are you?"

"Twenty-two."

"Wow. I'm the older woman. I'm twenty-six."

"Age is just a number. That's what Raquel says."

She knitted her eyebrows together and looked at him puzzled.

"My mother. She lives here in town and her boyfriend is this elderly gent. The silo painter."

"Ahhh! The cowboy. Heard all about him, and never actually met him. Oh, here's my brother. He always worries when I'm off fighting fires. He's a sweet lad."

Darren Jackson walked up to them, smiling broadly but looking Steve up and down. Close up, his deep-set eyes were a touch darker blue than his sisters' behind his eyeglasses, and he was slightly shorter than Steve. His face was angular under a mop of curly light brown hair and his thin lips were drawn tight. He had a large nose which was pointy at the tip, and overall, he was not much of a looker. He was clearly not happy seeing his big sister hanging out with the local Constable.

The death of their parents had left Darren Jackson with scars that would never heal. He took their deaths very hard but managed to finish high school with near perfect scores. You see, Darren was the ultimate triple threat in Brumby Flat. Not only was he the only plumber in town, he was also the local butcher and the odd jobs guy. With the third job, he got to know what was happening around him. All the sordid stuff. Locals often forgot he was in close proximity to them as he lay crouched behind bushes which badly needed trimming and their leaning front fences which he was busily mending. He was privy to all their dirty little secrets. He was a very smart lad with a high IQ of one hundred and thirty, and it was not unusual for him to play off waring families against each other. It was the best way he had to make a lot of money in a short time, and he certainly didn't want Constable Willaston to catch onto his scheming ways. His ultimate plan was to make as much money as he could and move to the city, away from Brumby Flat and the awful memories.

Kimberley enthusiastically introduced her brother to Steve Willaston.

Darren sniffed and twitched his nose, "Yeah. Good to meet you. Hey sis. Coming home for dinner tonight?"

She twisted a strand of her hair and said, "Yeah. Sure. I'm a bit too tired to cook. Been a long day, fighting the fire."

"Okay, I'll make us tea then."

"Great. What a wonderful little brother I have."

She then turned to Steve and flashed him a beguiling smile, "Darren, you don't mind if the Constable comes too? He looks like he could do with a good feed. His first fire, you know."

Steve smiled, "No. Really, it's okay. Another time maybe. It's been a long day for all of us."

As he turned to leave, he looked back at Kimberley and added with a sly wink, "You know where to find me, when you've thought about the other matter. Have a good evening."

Darren looked in puzzlement at his sister. She gave him a smug look in reply and said in a confident, low voice, "He likes me. A *lot*."

****

A familiar white station wagon pulled up in a quiet street within the township. Detective Duncan switched off the car engine, unbuckled his seatbelt and picked up his notebook which had been flung onto the passenger seat. He peered through the side window, his eyeglasses glinting in the bright midday sun. He let the windows down a fraction. He had a good back stretch and let out a big yawn.

He had spent the entire morning again being questioned in the local police station, but the new investigating unit had noted his story had remained unchanged since his last interview. He found it frustrating that he could not work on the case himself. He understood the reasoning, but he didn't like being the prime suspect in his own wife's murder.

He knew he should stay home as he had been put on leave from work, but he really wanted to follow the leads he had. No one was asking him if he had ideas or clues about Bette's killer.

He thought if he saw any suspicious behaviour conducted or implied by his list of suspects, he might be redeemed. He had parked himself outside of Anabella William's house. So far, all he could note down was the poor state of her front garden. The neat rows of cottage flower beds were long gone, overrun with weeds and prickles which sprayed over the cement footpaths.

He leant far back into the drivers' seat and closed his eyes for a long moment, feeling the warmth of sunlight reflected on his unshaven face. Then he looked down at his mobile phone which was resting on his lap. For a fleeting moment, he remembered Geena and a vision of her freckled naked body writhing on the bed came to life inside his head. He remembered finding her wearing a red Chinese silk dressing robe and little else. And how the garment had clashed so beautifully with her striking auburn hair.

He also remembered that he still had her number saved on his mobile phone. He was tempted to give her a call. Maybe physical female contact was exactly what he needed right now. He scrolled down the screen and found it. He stared at her name for a while. But he thought better of it and switched his mobile completely off. He felt ashamed for even thinking about her.

Suddenly, he heard clear footsteps coming up from behind. Through the rear-view mirror, he could see a middle-aged man walking along the footpath. He was wearing a beanie and dressed very casually in a red flannel shirt over black trackie pants which looked dusty around the knees.

The man suddenly stopped on the gravel pavement next to Duncan's car and looked at him, "Morning," he said brightly, giving a short wave too.

The stranger went to walk on by, but he stopped, turned around and looked hard again. Duncan smiled back slightly.

The pale, lined face frowned, "Hey mate, aren't you that detective guy?"

Duncan looked away quickly, clutching the steering wheel with both hands. He said nothing in return.

"Yeah, it's you," the man continued, but his voice suddenly rose in anger,

" You're in all the papers. You murdered your wife. Get outta here, mate. You got a nerve being here in town. Are you stalking someone else now? You gutless bloody wonder. Murderer!"

The man kept ranting on and he punched a fist in the air as Duncan turned on the ignition and rapidly sped off down the road, with tyres screeching. In the rear-view mirror, he could still see the man watching him go, shouting out a string of abusive words he could no longer hear.

Duncan drove on auto pilot, back to his home. When he finally parked in the driveway, put on the handbrake and switched off the ignition, he took off his glasses. He cried a couple of tears as he draped his arms over the top of the steering wheel and buried his head there.

"Oh man," he gasped, wiping them away furiously with his shirt sleeves, "I'm sorry Bette, I'm sorry."

Chapter Twelve

Raquel had finally opened the front door of the Raindrops Shop for business. The town was alive and busy again, buzzing with reporters, locals and curious strangers who had descended on it like blowflies to a backyard barbeque. She was not looking forward to being tied to the coffee machine for the next two hours, but deep down inside she knew that Bette would want the shop to be trading. She placed a few umbrellas on the porch with a set of water ski's positioned next to them.

She stood on the veranda for a moment, leaning against a post, thinking of her dear friend. She was dressed in a simple v neck white T-shirt and a denim skirt. She had popped over an apron to keep her clothes spotless and clean.

It didn't take long for the first reporters to wander inside, asking for their lattes, cappuccinos, and short black coffees. The pace was manageable. There was a steady stream of customers.

She did get a quiet interval of ten minutes where she sat down at one of the café tables and felt the inside pocket of her skirt. She had shoved an envelope with a handwritten note from Phil Proctor into it. She had found the envelope addressed to her on the dining table up at the cottage on the day of the fire. She stared at the envelope for a good minute and then tucked it away again into her skirt pocket. She was curious to see what he had written for her, but anxious about reading it at the same time. She had told him that she wasn't a fan of goodbyes and she guessed that writing the note was his clever way around it. But she didn't want to read any negative thoughts. She was thinking seriously about throwing the envelope into the rubbish bin. But for now, she left it in her pocket.

She was quite surprised when a couple from up York Peninsula way popped in and purchased a pair of snow boards.

She was even more surprised to see Duncan stride confidently into the shop after the last customers had left.

"Oh wow, you're here and the shop's open again!" he exclaimed, resting a fist on his right hip. He was casually attired, wearing a black T-shirt with his best tan trousers. His enforced semi-retirement seemed to suit him quite well.

"I think Bette would be happy about that."

He smiled and looked down briefly, "Yeah, for sure."

"Are you doing any follow up? Any leads?"

"Not really. I told you. I'm off the case now."

She wiped her damp hands on a tea towel and searched his face, "Okay. I know you're off the case. I get that, but I think you should do something. You're still under suspicion. The blame game all points to you."

He removed his glasses and rubbed them on a corner of his T-shirt, "I know. They won't leave me alone."

"Hey. I was thinking over something last night. Bette told me an interesting fact that night when she died."

Duncan's face changed to a look of hunger for retribution,

"What? What did she tell you?"

Raquel raised an index finger to her lips and walked past him, intent on closing the front door first. She firmly latched the door, then she turned on her heel to face him, "I know you will find this fact interesting. You know, Kitty is not the only blast from her past. Bette invited Kitty over for your wedding, as you know. But did you know this? There's someone else living here in town, who knew them both way back in Sydney. Back when they were all in high school together."

As she expected, Duncan leaned forward, intrigued, "Okay. Who is it?"

"The local high school principal."

Duncan pushed his glasses, which had slipped, back up the bridge of his nose, and nodded his head, "Well, he's new in town. I remember someone saying that," he said, walking around in a tight circle. He rubbed the back of his neck and was deep in his own thoughts, "Principal Reece Haddock. Okay. And how did he happen to know Bette and Kitty?"

"Bette said to me that he was a young teacher back at their old high school. She said she was shocked to find him here, now working as a high school principal. Now, isn't that a bit of a coincidence?"

Duncan was quiet for a few moments. She could see his intense blue eyes glinting behind the glasses.

"I'm probably going to shock you. But I need your help, Raquel. You have to get close to Reece Haddock and find out more about him. For me."

"Hang on. Wait on. I am not going to…spy on this man for you," she protested, "You're the detective."

"Yes, I was. Not my case anymore. But I need to find out more about him. Why is he here? Did he follow Bette here?

Don't you want to know the answers too? She was your friend."

"Of course. Yes, I do. But hey, I am not you. I'm not a detective. I don't know the right questions to ask the man. And okay. What if I say the wrong thing? And it turns out that he is Bette's killer. And what if, then he comes for me."

Duncan scoffed, "It's easy. You're over thinking it, Raquel. I'm not asking you to wear a wire and risk your life for me. No. Just find an opportunity and chat to the man. Keep it light-hearted, you know? Just a friendly, good old chat."

Raquel rolled her eyes and slapped her sides, "Oh right. How am I going to get that opportunity? My kid is like over six foot. He doesn't go to school anymore."

"It's very simple. I hate to say this, but I am fairly sure that he may even come to Bette's funeral. Whenever that will be. Or you could visit him at the school, give him your sympathy...because you know from Bette that he knew her and Kitty. You, see?"

"That could work. The second option. I don't want to think about the first one," she replied, in agreement with him. "And anyway, I wouldn't be telling him a lie. She did tell me this in the pub."

"Sorry. I know I shouldn't be asking you to do this, but you should be safe enough. You'll be at a high school. There's lots of people around."

Suddenly, Duncan slapped his forehead and heaved a loud sigh.

"What the hell am I doing? No forget it. Please don't do any of what I just said. It's not right."

"Understood. Thank you," she paused before continuing, "Now, we need to discuss the shop. I am keeping it open, but

I do expect to be paid for my time."

"Is it doing, okay?" he asked her straight out.

"Oh yes. Lots of coffees and umbrellas mainly. I haven't ordered any new stock as Bette kept it well stocked anyway. I just need to know what my wage is, going forward."

"Well, I am happy to give you about a third of the takings. I hope that's enough for you. We can talk more about it another day."

She shrugged her shoulders, "That sounds reasonable to me. I can't open every day, but I reckon I can at least cover four days. I guess you will close the Raindrops Shop eventually."

Duncan sighed heavily, "Not sure yet. For the moment, I think we'll just keep it going. I don't really feel I'm ready to deal with all this."

****

Raquel was seated rather uncomfortably in the main office of the Brumby Flat Secondary School. The chair had seen better days, maybe ten years ago, so she sunk deep down into its red vinyl upholstery. She was uncertain how she could get elegantly out of it when required. She was also not wearing the appropriate clothing to extract herself from it either, having chosen to wear a plain tight black pencil skirt with a fitted western check shirt.

The school secretary who was short and round with frizzy dyed orange hair, sat poised at the reception desk. She was peering at her over her reading glasses. She had explained to her that she had come to see Mr. Reece Haddock in relation to a mutual good friend, but the secretary wasn't very happy with that explanation. Raquel surmised she might be more than just his secretary. She was acting far too protective of the Principal's Office.

Raquel wasn't enjoying the experience and felt as awkward as when she was a high school student herself. She well remembered battling pimples, missing crucial assignment deadlines and making elaborate excuses to skip physical education classes. She wished that her genuine concern for Duncan's reputation hadn't talked her into connecting with Principal Reece Haddock.

Finally, the door on her left burst wide open and a middle-aged man with slightly peppered grey hair smiled down at her and thrust his right hand immediately forward. He was about her height, dressed in an ill-fitting grey suit. His reddish beard seemingly clashed with his salt and pepper hair.

He said in his strong voice, "Miss Willaston, is it? You knew Bette, is that right? Sharon said you had to see me rather urgently."

She smiled back and awkwardly arose from the chair which seemed to possess all who sat in it. She thrust out her hand and he shook it firmly, "Reece Haddock, it's lovely to meet you. Can we talk privately?"

He nodded his head, "Indeed, we can. Come into my office, please."

After he closed the door behind them, he walked around to the chair behind his desk. She slipped quietly into the chair opposite, turning to briefly admire his neat bookcase of textbooks and the framed diplomas on the side wall.

"I do remember Bette as Miss Bette Chiffley, you know."

"That was her name when you were teaching?"

"Yes. Now, what brings you so urgently to my office

today?"

Raquel shifted in her chair and took a deep breath. "I was told how close you were to both her and Kitty. Bette talked about the old school days at our last dinner together. So I have come here to give you my condolences. I thought we could at least comfort each other. Through hard times, you know?"

Haddock looked uncomfortable and averted his eyes. He shuffled a few papers around on his desk and said in a low, considered voice, "That's very kind of you, Miss Willaston. Her death has shocked me greatly. Shocked us all in town, I believe. I hope that poor Kitty will be okay and recovers well. Has the funeral been planned?"

"No, not as yet."

"I will certainly go to her funeral."

She refocused on her questioning of him, "So, your last meeting with Bette, I guess you talked about the past."

"We certainly did. How Magda became a fashion model. Kitty. As you know her as. We talked about her marriages. Past and in the present tense at the time. It was just a good, solid catch up. She was a lovely, kind girl."

It was time for Raquel to delve further, so she leaned forward.

"You know, Mr. Haddock. I think it's a very strange coincidence that you end up working in the same town as Bette. All these years later."

He smiled and tapped a pen on his desk, "Ah yes. A lot can happen in ten years, twenty years even. I'm sure you've had some amazing coincidences in your time. Not impossible."

"I am sorry. But can you understand how it might look to an outsider? Like me?"

"I can explain it. You see, I was a young teacher over twenty years ago and I have worked hard to become a School Principal. It was hard work and completely by accident, here I am, in Brumby Flat. I didn't have much choice where I could go and a vacancy came up here. And believe me, it was by accident, certainly not by design, my dear."

"Bette also mentioned to me their third friend at school. Dead long ago now. Mandy-Jane Fischer."

Mr. Haddock also leaned forward across his desk, his sunspot ravaged right hand concealing his left.

"I remember Mandy-Jane, but not as well. I know she drowned in a local reservoir. It was all over the news. It was a tragic end for such a promising young woman. They said she was murdered but I believe they never found her killer."

Raquel went quiet and stood up to leave. It was then that she finally noticed photographs hanging next to his diplomas on the same wall. She remembered that Bette had noticed a photograph of Haddock as a young teacher standing next to Mandy-Jane and had told her all about it.

"I feel that you are looking for complications where there isn't any, Miss Willaston," he said drily, "Now then. Are you moonlighting as a detective? Or are you just plain curious?"

She turned her head, but said nothing in response to that. In her mind, she was busy cursing Duncan for putting her into that position.

He leant back, hard against his chair and cleared his throat loudly. He could see she wasn't going to answer any questions that he had. An uncomfortable silence descended, and Reece realised that he would have to break the spell of it himself.

"Well, thank you for coming over and chatting to me. I will miss her, of course. Our reacquaintance was far too short."

She stood there and studied the two framed photographs more closely but did not see what Bette had said was there. However, she observed there was an empty picture hook in the middle. Her studious gaze was not missed by Reece Haddock.

She smiled at his now narrowed hazel eyes, "Yes, I get that. I will miss her too. She was my first real friend in town. When I moved here."

"Well, enjoy your day. Stay safe, Miss Willaston," he said in a tone she wasn't quite sure of.

He got out of his office chair, opened the door for her like an old-fashioned gentleman would, and very gently closed the door after her. He heard his secretary Sharon's sharp, pitchy voice and then the sound of another door being shut a couple of seconds later.

When he was certain she had left the school grounds, he finally leaned his broad back against his door and closed his eyes for a few seconds. His right hand visibly shook slightly as he smoothed it over his finely peppered hair. He patted his shirt collar down and pulled at his auburn beard.

The school bell rang for morning recess, permeating through the walls of the main building. It brought him back to the realities of being a high school Principal.

He pushed his finger down on the intercom, "Sharon, make sure I am not disturbed for a bit. No. Actually, bring your tablet in with you."

The school secretary entered his office a moment later, peering at him over her reading glasses.

Reece rose from his desk, "Lock the door," he instructed, in a low, commanding voice. She fumbled with the latch until it clicked over.

"Sharon, I need you to take dictation."

She blinked a few times, smiled slightly, opened the top button of her frilly neck blouse and then replied in her pitchy voice, "Okay, you'll have to drop your trousers."

Reece obliged her.

She stepped forward and rested the tablet on his desk, hitched up her skirt an inch or two and bent down on all fours. Her head of fizzy orange hair disappeared under his desk, as indeed half her body. A satisfied look slowly spread across his broad face as she quietly went to work.

Chapter Thirteen

It was a warm Sunday morning and Raquel had decided to sleep in. She had slipped her dressing gown on and was walking barefoot towards her kitchen to make herself a quick cuppa, when she heard loud knocking at her front door. She had wanted to return to bed. She grumbled under her breath and peered through the flyscreen door. Duncan had appeared on her front doorstep again.

"Oh. It's you again. This is becoming a worrying trend," Raquel said with a sharp dose of sarcasm. She unlocked the flyscreen door with a show of reluctance and let him squeeze his way in.

He stood tall in her loungeroom, dressed casually again in a black turtleneck skivvy and tan trousers. He smirked, his eyes twinkling, "Good morning. I had to rush over to give you the news. I got a message about it."

"Oh yeah. What's new? What's so urgent, Phil?"

"She's awakened."

Raquel frowned and then raised an eyebrow, "Oh. Right. You're saying Kitty Caulfield is out of the coma."

"Spot on. And guess who is going to pay her a little visit?"

"Oh great. You. You're back on the case!" she exclaimed excitedly.

"No, no, no. It's you," he pointed to her with his index finger, "I can't turn up at the hospital. But you have the golden ticket. You're the other bridesmaid. And you have the best chance to find out, maybe, what happened to her at the wedding reception."

"Look Phil. You know that Kitty hates me. She won't tell me a thing."

"Oh yeah. She'll talk to you. You are her connection to Bette, you see. You were her bridesmaids. Of course, she'll talk to you."

At the mention of his dead wife's name, Duncan paused for a few moments, a lump in his throat. Then he continued.

"Look. I really need to know what happened. Who was with her? I'm sure she didn't just fall into the dam. She's going to be so happy to see you. I am sure that she will take you into her confidence."

"I wish you had someone else to ask," she tightened her dressing gown across her body and indicated to a pile of books on her coffee table, "I was planning to do nothing, but catch up on my reading. It's piling up."

He arched an eyebrow, "Oh. What are you reading?"

"Crime fiction. Probably your influence."

She studied the hurt visible in Duncan's vivid blue eyes and realised she had to rearrange her plans. The pile of books would have to remain untouched.

"Okay. But Phil, I don't know what to ask her. You should be doing your own research."

"You'll be right. Just act natural. Be your natural, curious self, Raquel. Don't force yourself onto the poor woman. Just let her open up to you."

"Like a flower?"

He shrugged his shoulders, "Not an analogy I would tend to use, but yes, okay. Like a flower. Ask her how she is feeling and does she remember anything. Will you please go and visit her?"

She made a face but nodded her head, "If it's for Bette, I will. I'm not working today. I can't believe you are getting me to do this. But this is it. Last time I'm sticking my neck out."

He smirked and said, "I have complete faith in you."

"Let's be clear. I'm doing this for Bette's sake. Not for you. I'll get changed and drive there soon. What room number or section do I find her in?"

He took a small crumbled up piece of paper out of his trouser back pocket and handed it directly to her.

She was not a fan of visiting sick people in hospital, but once again, she was doing this for her dead best friend. She closed the front door, as Duncan turned away. She walked into her cluttered bedroom and quickly changed into her favourite floral dress. She stopped to admire her reflection in the bathroom and touched up her make up in the dressing table mirror. If she was going to visit Kitty Caulfield the model, she wanted to at least look her very best.

She drove into the city and found the parking to be the most difficult part of her journey. The hospital carpark was full, and she had to drive around for ten minutes before someone reversed out of their carpark space. She shot into the park and checked the car mirror one more time to make sure she looked good enough for Kitty. Then, after glancing down at the piece of paper Duncan had provided her with, she made her way to the hospitals' main entrance.

She had to walk along two long corridors and catch two

separate lifts to find the ward where Kitty was.

She entered through the sliding doors with some apprehension. She had never seen a person who had been in a coma before, so she didn't know what to expect. She came up to the nurses' station and asked about Kitty Caulfield. The young nurse regarded her under her blonde fringe, and as she was about to start her rounds, she had removed a pen from her shirt pocket. She was all about her job.

"Are we a friend or family?"

"Yes, a friend definitely. How is she doing?"

She tapped her pen impatiently on the counter, "Thankfully lucid. She's in room twelve. Sign in here at the desk please. Your name, address and phone number."

Raquel obliged, removing her own pen from the depths of her handbag. She then glanced down the long corridor and noticed a policeman positioned near the door. That was something Duncan had not warned her about. She took a deep intake of breath and quickly filled in her personal information. She had managed to pass the first hurdle, but could she make it past the cop?

She smiled at him as she approached, but he was only interested in one detail.

"Did you sign in?"

"Yes, I did."

"You have five minutes with the patient. She's apparently very weak."

She walked into the room and found Kitty on her own, in a hospital room which had three empty beds. She was sprawled on her back on a hospital bed, looking paler and even thinner than she remembered her being. Her slender left arm was connected to a drip. Her long dark hair was twisted in a side ponytail, looped over her right shoulder. Her head was propped up on a thin white pillow. She opened her pale green eyes and blinked several times, like she was trying to focus on Raquel and work out who she was. Raquel noticed the dark hollows around her eyes. She wore no makeup but despite her face being a blank canvas she still looked like a million dollars. She could stand up in her hospital gown and twirl around on a catwalk and still look model material perfect.

"Hey Kitty, it's me, Bette's other crazy bridesmaid," Raquel announced with a little wave of her hand, hoping she didn't sound nervous.

Kitty widened her eyes and half smiled back at her, "Well, I am happy to see you again," she said in her clipped strange accent. "Is it true? They've told me I've been out of it for a while. I feel dreadful. How do I look? I must look absolutely frightful."

"You don't look the best," she lied. She grabbed a chair from the corner of the room and set it down closer to the bed. She eased herself carefully into it.

"Oh, thank God. I hope you can fill in some details for me. I missed the entire wedding reception, I think. Bette must be really mad with me."

Her last statement hit Raquel particularly hard. It was then that she realised that Kitty had no idea that Bette Duncan was dead. And she knew it was not her place to tell her either.

"Not really. I remember you were there at the reception most of the time. But I think you went off, on your own. But that was later."

Raquel noticed an attractive bloom of wildflowers in a large vase at Kitty's bedside. She inclined her head towards them.

"Beautiful flowers."

Kitty smiled slightly, "Aren't they gorgeous? They're from my darling publicist Kathy Meadows. She wants to know when I'll be back in Sydney for modelling assignments. I'm a bit too weak, but as soon as I can stand up, I'm out of here."

Kitty propped herself up on an elbow and winched at the pain of her sudden exertion.

"Bloody hell. Damn it!" she exclaimed. "I don't remember anything. Well, not much. It's like everything went black. Anyway, why are you here again?"

"Just visiting you. I thought I'd say hello and…maybe you need something."

"You know what I'd like? I really need to get out of here. I keep getting questioned by the police, but I honestly don't remember what happened that night,"

"You must remember something, Kitty. Even a small detail."

She shrugged her shoulders and lay her head back down on the pillow. She was quiet for half a minute, partially closing her eyes.

"It's really hard, Rachel."

"I'm Raquel."

"Oh right. Yes, you are. I just remember bits and pieces. I remember I went to that water hole to meet someone."

"Dam," Raquel corrected her.

"Yes, that's right. I met this man at the dam. I remember I was on a dating app. This man responded to my messages. So, I went to meet him outside and then, well. It all goes black, right there. I don't remember anything else, but I had this overwhelming feeling of fear and there's lots of darkness around me."

"He was a stranger then."

She shook her head, "No. I am fairly sure that we had met somewhere before. He knew me, I think. I mean, of course he would. I am a famous model, you know, but I was comfortable being with him. And then, I just don't remember what happened next. That's the problem."

" Don't worry about it, Kitty. It will take some time. Be patient with yourself."

She touched her forehead, "Yes, you're right. I mean I was in a coma for nearly a month. I think that's what they told me. I'm very lucky to be alive. The doctor said that to me. How scary is that?"

"Very."

Kitty stared at her suddenly, her green eyes narrowing suspiciously, "Rachel. Remind me why you are here to see me again?"

"I'm Raquel. I am here to say hello and of course, ask if you need anything."

She sighed and waved her pale hand dismissively, "I'm alright. Just sick of being among sick people and being connected to this dreary drip thing. I so want to get out. I also need a smoke badly."

Raquel frowned and said, "But I haven't seen you smoke. Bette always said you were clean living."

"My dear, I very nearly died out there. I think I deserve and need a cigarette for my nerves."

"Do you want me to sneak out and bring you back a packet?"

Kitty's eyes sparkled for a moment, "Would you be so

kind, dear? I've got my purse somewhere. It's okay. I'll pay you back, not a worry."

She waved her hand, "Nah. It's okay. On me."

"Before you go. Rachel," Kitty held out a pale slender hand, "Could you please do me another small favour?"

Raquel nodded her head.

"Just tell Bette, my beautiful bestie that I am so sorry for ruining her wedding celebrations. I must've caused so much turmoil for her. Please, please. Give her all my love."

"Yes, I will. I promise."

The nurse suddenly appeared at the doorway, holding a clipboard, "Sorry, visiting time is finished now. If you can come back another day."

Raquel got up and had a little stretch, "Okay. Well, I'll drop in another time."

"Oh. What about the…"

Kitty noticed the nurse frown at her. She realised that she wasn't going to get any cigarettes.

"I'll come back another time. See you then," Raquel had to repeat herself.

Chapter Fourteen

Working on the tenth chai latte for the morning, Raquel stopped for a moment and wiped a bead of sweat from her forehead. It was another scorcher of a day in Brumby Flat. She had opened the shop again to trade. She was happy that, for a change, Duncan had not made an appearance. In an effort to stay cool, she was wearing the same wrap dress and flats she had worn to Proctor's picnic. She hid it under her work apron.

Her heart soared when the new real estate agent walked right through the front door. He wasn't in his suit and tie this time, but it was forty-one degrees in the shade. He was sensibly outfit in a fine check western shirt and low slung tight tan trousers. And they were suitably tight.

Sullivan O'Grady grew up in the district. His family had farmed their thirty-hectare property for over six decades. He had an older brother, but they were like chalk and cheese. His brother Adrian was shorter, had darker skin and he was stocky in statue. His facial features were more chipped by an axe handle, rather than finely chiselled as his younger brothers were. Even their own mother could see Sullivan was different from the lot of them. She often said to him, shaking her head, "You're not made for farmin', love. You're made for much bigger things."

And girls flocked to him always and it caused him a lot of grief. But he loved the ladies. His handsome features and perfect physique dictated his early job choices after dropping out of high school in year eleven. He was not academically bright, but he was brilliant at sports. He excelled at athletics, tennis and swimming.

His first job was as a junior sales assistant at the local hardware store. He knew nothing about fixing stuff, tools or how to use them. A spanner particularly puzzled him. However, his manager was quick to realise the handsome kid was a revelation. He brought the women of the town flocking into the store. They all wanted to talk to young Sullivan and buy their tools, paint and anything else in the store direct from him. Even a bag of chicken feed was okay for ladies who didn't even own a chicken. They would sell it online later or to a friend who really owned chickens.

It was noticed twelve months after his employment, that renovation work across the town had increased by forty per cent. On weekends, the sounds of hammering and drilling, mainly attributed to the erection of pergolas, timber decking and shedding reverberated across the township. Meanwhile, he was busy keeping up his tennis practise and being active in local swimming competitions.

Bored with his job after a few years, Sullivan then moved up to the sunny Gold Coast in Queensland and served as a Surf Lifeguard for a year. He very quickly got tired of plucking besotted schoolgirls out of shallow water who were pretending to drown and quit. Then he was a bartender at a posh island resort, but this proved difficult as well. He soon got sick of married women squeezing his shapely bum and others slipping him spare keys to their rooms. That job also lasted a year.

He had a chance meeting with an Indian film producer while he was propping up a bar in Cairns, drinking away his lady problems. The producer enthusiastically told him he would be a perfect fit in a Bollywood movie, with his film star looks. Sullivan had some savings behind him, so he headed off to India to pursue a new dream. He had never danced before, but he was athletic and confident that he could learn. He enthusiastically booked in some dancing lessons, employed an acting coach and put his name down with a Mumbai based casting agent. He was advised to change his surname to a Hindi name, let his curly hair grow a bit more, tell casting directors that he had a trickle of Indian blood on his father's side and told to learn some basic Hindi.

He struggled in Bollywood for a couple of years, achieving a close up or two dancing in some big musical sequences. He was all hands waving and spinning about in the air and all too often, his feet were pointed in the opposite direction of the other dancers. However, his handsome face, natural sandy hair and easy-going nature kept him employed. He was usually positioned in the back row of dancers, so his uncoordinated, windmill style dance moves were not so apparent to the Indian movie going audiences. But certainly, he did not get the acting roles he was told he would easily achieve.

Finally conceding defeat and down to his last few hundred rupees, he flew back home and retreated to the family farm for a bit. Even helped out his old man with the harvest. He had his feet up on the dashboard, busy tapping away on a dating app, while the harvester followed the GPS map and crop-gathered its way across the paddocks.

One day, Sullivan had his big lightbulb moment while reading the local newspaper. He wasn't a big reader but that particular morning, he perused a number of real estate listings and thought to himself this is something he could do. He had the gift of the gab. He enrolled in an online real estate course part time, and he only just managed to pass. He rented a shop in the main street as his office and started work almost immediately. He had three listings in town in the first week and five ladies called him for private viewings. At least one had money and bought one of the properties. It proved to be a promising start.

Sullivan smiled disarmingly at Raquel and leaned over the shop counter, a lock of his sandy hair curling over his right cheek. He definitely had a smooth way about him, which made her feel like she had his full attention.

"Hello. A coffee please," he smiled, leaning so close she could see the tiny amber flecks in his soft brown eyes.

"Hey Sullivan, good to see you. What sort you after?

"A cap is okay by me. And how are you doing today?"

"I am doing alright," she nodded her head and passed on a coffee to another customer who was waiting impatiently beside him.

"You haven't come up to see me at my office, like you've promised me," he remarked.

"I made you no such promise. I've had a lot of things on my plate. One day. How's your business going? Got many houses to sell?"

Sullivan shrugged his shoulders. "Look, I've just started here. Gotta couple on the market but I'm hearing some people in town are nervous. You know, after the hit and run, and the girl in the dam. So, I've got some appraisals coming up soon."

Raquel made a face, "Oh wow. You reckon some people will actually leave town?"

"I think that will happen. Plus, that recent fire. Forgot that part. Yeah, mate. People here are nervy. By the way, it's gotta be a takeaway cap. I have to go soon. Love to chat longer with you. But seeing a client this morning."

"Oh excellent. Sounds like you're doing well."

He gave her a wink, a huge thumbs up motion and finally, slapped the countertop with a tune, "Touch wood, yeah. I like this town. I have no competition."

"I guess you don't. The next nearest agency is way down the road."

He flashed her a wide grin and a little wink, "Far enough away. I bet you don't know this about me. I am doing alright because I came from Brumby Flat. My family owned a farm in the district for over sixty years."

She smiled, "Okay, I guess that makes you a dinky-di local."

"Too right."

She finished his coffee with a flurry and handed it to him. He felt for his wallet in his back pocket, but she shook her head and waved her hand.

"It's on the house."

He grinned and headed for the front door, "Thanks for that. Catch up with you later on."

Outside Sullivan had a quick sip of the chai latte and nodded his head approvingly. He was surprised that it wasn't half bad. He jumped into his midnight blue V8 with the big spoiler and roared down the road. He was running a few minutes late to see John Templeton-Moore.

He had never imagined that old Templeton-Moore would sell his modest timber frame house in town. He received the phone call earlier that morning, where the old man was sounding very upset, saying he needed to sell his home 'desperately and fast'. He said to come over and see him before he left town for good.

The house was just two streets down, so he was there in two seconds flat. He used his rear-view mirror to tidy up the neckline of his western check shirt. He grabbed his clipboard from the passenger seat and climbed out. He opened the low wire gate and stood at the front door which was wide open. It was not ajar or unlocked, the door was actually open. He thought it was a bit unusual, even for a trusting country person. Sullivan hesitated for a moment before peering inside.

"Hello? John?" he yelled out.

There was no answer.

He stepped forward into the hallway, and made a floorboard creak under his shoe's heel. "John? It's me, Sullivan."

He stood there, listening hard and was sure someone was in the house. But he wasn't sure if it was Templeton-Moore.

He yelled out again, "It's Sullivan, and I bought someone else along with me."

He lied because he was feeling uneasy.

Then he heard it. A blood curdling scream came from the back, followed by a slamming door. He froze for a moment. Then he dropped his clipboard of paperwork, papers spiralling to the floor at his feet. He shot down the hallway, straight into the kitchen.

He found Templeton-Moore gasping for air and lying on the floor, his throat partially cut, and three fingers of his right hand cut clean right through. The back door was closed but the screen door was creaking back and forth on its' hinges. Someone had left in a hurry. There was a trail of blood leading all the way to the back door. The floor was littered with knives which had fallen from their positions in a toppled over knife block on the kitchen island bench.

"Oh Christ," Sullivan went down on his right knee, bent over Templeton-Moore, who stared up at him with wide, frightened eyes. He tried to talk but no sound came out. His head was lying back in a small pool of blood.

"Don't move mate. Stay cool."

Sullivan whipped out the mobile phone in his back pocket and dialled the emergency number quickly, "Yeah, I need an ambulance now to Brumby Flat. The address is…"

****

Raquel trudged up the footpath to Proctor's old cottage in the heat of the day. She had promised to clean it up for the McCarthy's. They had called her again and said that Proctor and his father had left it untidy, especially the kitchen and the bathroom. Along the way, she stopped at the local petrol station and bought the days newspaper to read when she had a spare minute. She was dressed to work, wearing a simple denim skirt, teamed with a white T-shirt.

She unlocked the front door and peered down the hallway. So far so good. She walked to the kitchen and noticed the smell right away. The rubbish bin had not been emptied and the double sink was piled full of dirty dishes untouched.

"Oh crap," she signed, hands on hip. She looked for a mop and bucket and other cleaning materials to use. Finding none, she had to return to her car and bring in the cleaning gear she had brought with her.

Returning to the kitchen, she snapped on her pink rubber gloves and put out the smelly rubbish first. Then she started mopping the floor. She left the dirty dishes in the sink for last.

She snapped off the rubber gloves and decided to have a short break before facing the bathroom. She left the horrors in store for her in there as a complete surprise.

She picked up the newspaper from the kitchen bench and took it into the dining room. She sat at the dining table and brushed her hair out of her eyes. The first page got her immediate attention. It was about Brumby Flat again. A local man had been attacked in his home by an unknown intruder brandishing a knife.

She started to read when a shadow moved across her left shoulder. She jumped and turned around to find her son Steve standing above her, staring back at her.

He was dressed in his policeman's uniform.

"God. You scared the crap out of me," she gasped, clutching her chest.

"Sorry Raquel. I sneaked in through the back door. You know, you shouldn't be up here on your own. And the door should've been locked."

"What are you on about?" she rolled her shoulders.

He shook his head, leaned over and tapped the front page with his forefinger. He slumped down into the chair opposite her, removing his hat, "This happened yesterday. It's not safe to be here anymore."

"Okay. Let me read it, honey, for myself."

She rustled the paper and scanned the front-page headlines.

Her focus returned to the article she had noticed before, 'Farmer bashed in Brumby' it proclaimed.

She read the first few lines of the story and then folded it over, to peer back at her son.

"Awful news, isn't it? But it happens anywhere. Not just here in Brumby Flat."

Her son rolled his eyes and banged his right fist against the tabletop in a show of frustration, "Can't believe this. Don't you see? Don't you get it? There's a crazed killer running around town again. John Templeton-Moore would be dead, if his would be killer wasn't disturbed. You have to lock all your doors or leave town. I can't protect everyone."

"Hey. You don't need to yell at me."

He looked down at his hands, his eyebrows knotted in a frown, and Raquel then understood how deeply upset he really was. She reached out and gently patted his right hand.

"Spill it. Just tell me what's really wrong," she said quietly.

"I'm a cop, I uphold the law, but I feel powerless to protect the town from this threat. And people are going to leave here. Yankee Tanaka called me earlier. She told me her family are leaving town. They're moving into the city. Putting their home on the market and just going. Like, straight away."

"You can only do your best. Don't beat yourself up."

Steve bit his top lip and nodded, "I know. I know. But I like her, mum."

She widened her eyes. He had never called her mum before. Not that she could remember.

"She's young. She's confusing as hell. I don't know. I can't get her out of my head sometimes."

"I get that. Love makes no sense or reason. Anyway, yeah,

I'll lock my doors. But I am not leaving town and Phil Duncan's still around."

"Don't tell me you still trust him?"

"True. He's not my favourite person in the world but look. We're all human. We all make mistakes. But he's not the killer type. He saved us all two years ago from Sandy Mitchell. Well, saved me and Bette, and Proctor too."

"Yeah, I remember. Please. Just be wary of him. Your friend died in strange circumstances. Still under investigation."

"I know. Sullivan O'Grady found this local guy. Says here he was 'bashed within an inch of his life.' Awful. Poor young Sullivan must be really shaken up."

Suddenly her mobile phone rang, and she recognised the number right away. She placed it immediately back into her skirt pocket.

"Aren't you going to take it?" he asked.

"Not really. Nothing important."

It was Duncan. She had a strong feeling that he was contacting her about the latest incident, and she wasn't prepared to talk about any of it in front of Steve.

"I might go and see Sullivan, see how he's coping."

"Might be a good idea. Didn't realise you knew him so well."

"He comes into the shop. Likes my coffee. That's it."

"Not your new relationship, is he?"

She smirked and waved her hand dismissively, "No. no. Definitely not. He's nice eye candy only. Look. I had a long, tough run with Phil Proctor, so I think I deserve a break from relationships."

Steve smiled, "Oh yeah. And I've got a date tonight.

Could be the start of a new relationship for me."

"Oh, tell me. Tell me."

"If it goes well, you'll be the first to know. Please lock that door when I leave."

****

Kimberley Ann Jackson sat waiting nervously in the dimly lit Spur and Fetlock hotel's beer garden. She batted her hand at the fifteenth mosquito which had landed on her fleshy neck and pricked it for her blood.

She was out of her Firie uniform, wearing a strapless floral pantsuit with her ash blonde hair curled over her bare left shoulder. She wore only a little makeup, just enough to show off her pale blue eyes and some pale pink lippy. She finished her polished look with two shiny gold bangles on her left wrist.

Her date was already ten minutes late. She frowned as she studied her watch under the poor lighting.

Waiting staff walked past her and she was tempted to ask them for a drink, but she decided to wait for her date to arrive.

Steve Willaston finally appeared, still wearing his policeman's uniform which he wore well. He knew it too. He smiled and nodded at his date. He heaved a sigh of relief to himself when he saw her. He had looked for her in the dining room and thought she had stood him up.

She smiled back, showing off the attractive dimple in her right cheek. She got up and bent her cheek forward, which he kissed briefly, and he held her sides for a fleeting moment.

"Hey, are you trying hard to really impress me?" she asked in her voice which sounded like music to his ears.

"What do you mean?" he asked, pulling out his chair to take a seat opposite her.

"You're in your uniform still."

"Sorry. I came straight from work unfortunately. Half the town's gone crazy with the whiff of murder. I'm sorry but I can only stick around for a quick meal. Have to change out of my uniform soon."

She passed him the new flashy pub menu, "So that's convenient. A quick dinner. And will everything else be so quick, Constable?"

He rolled his shoulders and his lopsided smile reappeared, "I like things to go at a slower pace actually. Now, wow, you look amazing tonight."

"I wasn't going to wear *my* uniform. As nice and sexy as it is," she giggled.

"You'd look good in a blanket."

She giggled again.

"Oh, I'm sorry. That came out completely wrong," he said, feeling suddenly shy and silly.

"Oh no. It's okay. I like the Freudian slip. Honestly, I do."

"I was trying to say it wouldn't matter what you wear. You look so perfect anyway."

Her wide blue eyes danced under the dim glow of the cheap outdoor string lights. Even her face, although partially covered in shadow, he could see how beautiful and natural she was.

He leaned his face over the table and reached out to hold her warm right hand in his own.

"That's nice of you to say."

"I am only saying what's true."

She pushed her hair off her face and said, "Should we

order our meals and drinks?"

"I guess we go inside to order. I haven't been here before."

"To be honest, Constable Willaston, I'm not that hungry."

"Steve," he corrected her, squeezing her hand gently.

"Well, Steve. It's so crowded inside, I had to get this table outside and I have lost count how many times I've been bitten by the mozzies. I'd much rather hang out with you and talk basically."

He smiled again, "As long as that's what you want. I have to admit, I am happy with that too. I want to get to know you."

"What about the tall, slim girl? Kristina Tanaka? Are you still hooked on her?"

He shook his head, "No, all good. she wasn't my type at all. I've just told you. I really like you."

"Hmm. Older woman with a younger man. Can that work out?" she teased.

"I am willing to learn all the ropes you throw at me."

She leaned back against her chair, her breasts tantalisingly thrust forward in her strapless pantsuit. Steve was finding it increasingly difficult to keep his eyes focused just on her pretty face.

"Steve, I think we should explore all possibilities."

They left the table and the hotel together, arm in arm, talking and laughing like they had known one another for years. Within twenty-four hours, Steve's memory of Kristina 'Yankee' Tanaka had faded into a folkloric existence.

Chapter Fifteen

Duncan turned his car off the dark freeway and drove up the hill with high beams still on. He parked his white station wagon at the Topham Hill lookout and switched off the engine. He sat back in the drivers' seat, overlooking the twinkling lights of the town on one side and the bushland covered in a blanket of darkness on the other. Raquel was seated in the passenger seat, admiring the same scenery. He lowered the car window and rested an arm over the rim.

"I don't understand why we have to come up here again?" she remarked.

"Of course, you wouldn't," he breathed so deeply, she could hear him over the chirping sound of crickets and the soft buzz of mosquitoes.

"We're perfectly alone up here. It's the safest spot for us to swap notes and observations," he replied.

"Well, I don't like being up here. In the dark."

"Because of your wandering mind, no doubt."

"No. I feel more like I am being used," she said quietly, looking down at her hands which were folded on her lap.

Duncan rubbed his forehead, realising that she wasn't in a joking frame of mind. He grabbed her right hand tenderly into his own, half turning his body in the drivers' seat to look at her. His hand was warm and once again, she felt an involuntary shiver arise from his touch to her inner being. As much as she wanted to reclaim her hand, she was content to just leave it there.

"Look. Don't think that way, please. I appreciate the trouble you are going to, for Bette. I wish…I was able to investigate. I don't want my back against the wall, in case more people are in danger. Especially you."

She inclined her head in acknowledgment, "I know what you are trying to do. But this is getting complicated. I didn't get much in the way of helpful information for you. I saw Kitty who still hates me by the way. And I met with Mr. Haddock who is now very suspicious of me."

"What? You saw him? Wow. I said not to."

"I did it for Bette."

"Go on. Fill me in."

He let go of her hand.

"Yes, I will. I'm just sick of the lies they're publishing about you. They're painting you out to be a monster."

Duncan leant forward and played with a lock of her hair, rolling it between his thumb and forefinger. She felt her heart race a little. He didn't seem to be aware he was even doing it. She noticed that he had a faraway look in his eyes. His voice came out deeper but lower in tone somehow.

"Thanks for believing in me. I appreciate it. Anyway, go on. Tell me."

"Sure. In a nutshell, Kitty doesn't remember much, except she did say she was certain that the person she was with at the dam, it was someone she knew. She hooked up with them on some dating app. I could see she was struggling to remember things."

Duncan nodded, dropped his hand from her hair and started cleaning his glasses again, "Well, that's interesting."

"Now, Mr. Reece Haddock, well, he was even more interesting. Bette had told me about the framed photo of him with Mandy-Jane in his office. You'd remember about her. She was that high school friend of theirs who drowned in a reservoir. That photo was suddenly missing. It wasn't there in the office. He was hiding something for sure, and he thought I was acting like a detective. I think I overdid the questioning, just a little bit. And that's all your fault."

"Too late now. Can't change his opinion," he said.

She went quiet, rethinking about the days' events.

"So, what do you think about the recent bashing? That poor farmer."

"I think," Duncan drew out his words, "there's a bad element in town, which needs to be stamped out quickly. Might not be related to Kitty or Bette. Maybe."

Suddenly, her mobile phone started to vibrate like mad in her jeans pocket. She whipped it out and looked at the screen. She showed him the name on the screen, and it made Duncan raise an eyebrow. She indicated to him that she would take the call outside the car. She stepped out into the balmy night air and answered the call as brightly as she could. She only took four steps away from the car because it was nearly pitch-black outside.

"Hey. Hello Anabella. What a nice surprise to hear from you. How are you?"

She could hear no answer.

"Hello?"

"Yes, yes, I am here. I am so sorry, so very sorry," she replied, her voice low and it sounded like she was crying.

"Anabella. Are you okay? What's wrong?"

"I really need to talk to you. Can I see you tomorrow at the shop?"

Raquel thought for a moment as gravel made a scrunching sound under her flat shoes, "I'm working elsewhere. I won't be at the shop until the afternoon. We can talk over the phone now, if you want to. I have some free time now."

"No, no. I really must see you, Raquel. It's rather urgent."

"Oh well, okay. I'll see you maybe two o'clock."

The line went quiet again and she heard distinct sobbing.

Eventually she heard Anabella say, "Oh good. Please don't forget. We must talk urgently."

"Okay. That's fine. See you tomorrow."

The call finished abruptly. Raquel stared at the screen for a time and then walked slowly back to Duncan's car. It was a very odd phone call, she thought to herself.

She slipped back into the passenger seat with Duncan still half turned towards her, his arm casually draped over the back of his car seat. His right leg was curled against the steering wheel. He did not look totally comfortable, his body twisted in that way.

"What was that all about? What did Anabella Williams want with you?"

"It was a strange call."

He smirked and rolled his shoulders, "Why was it strange? What did she say to you?"

"Firstly, I forgot that she even had my phone number."

Duncan nodded his head, listening intently.

"Also, she said she had to see me urgently. It sounded like she had been crying."

"Maybe she's got man trouble? She's still a looker, that

one. I thought I saw her wearing a catsuit the other day. Leather boots up to her knees too. Bloody hell. I had to look twice at her. Never mind."

Raquel frowned at him, "I don't know if that's what it is. Anyway, I'll meet her in the shop tomorrow. I suppose I'll find out what's upset her so much."

"Let me know if you need my help."

"Phil. You might be right. Maybe it's just girl talk. But she's a mature woman, you know."

He lifted his hands up in the air. "You have your problem, I have mine. I'm going to keep an eye on Haddock. I think you're right about him. He's definitely hiding something."

"How are you going to watch him? You can't."

"I will chat to Longmeil about that. Maybe he'll listen to me. Someone has to listen."

Raquel nodded, "Don't drop my name into the conversation."

"Thanks for sticking your neck out."

He took her hand up again and squeezed it gently, but firmly.

"It's okay. But like I said before, that's it. Not doing any more of your bloody work for you, Phil."

****

Anabella Williams finally breezed through the front door of the Raindrops Shop. Raquel was starting to lose her patience waiting, as it was nearly closing time when she made her appearance.

However, she found she couldn't be angry with Anabella. Her slavish devotion to recreating an era never disappointed.

Anabella was wearing her new vintage best, a short floral shift dress with knee high white boots and a black patent leather handbag on her wrist. Her hair was piled high in a perfect salt and pepper beehive, and she had a peace symbol necklace bouncing across her chest. Raquel thought she was paying homage to the Woodstock music festival. Although she was no spring chicken, Anabella still had the trim figure and the right attitude to carry off the youthful look. To finish off her immaculate appearance, she wore a bright orange polish on her naturally long curved fingernails.

"Sorry I'm a bit late. I was at the hairdressers for longer than I expected," she said very apologetically. Her makeup was dark and smudged and the long false eyelashes seemed to be hindering her vision. She went to put her purse down on a café table, but it missed and fell straight to the floor.

Raquel scooped it up and placed it safely on the tabletop for her. Then she tried to find the chair and nearly missed that too. Raquel fortunately steered her a little to the right by grabbing her left elbow.

"I had something urgent to tell you. I'm so sorry about this. I feel so much shame."

Raquel removed her apron with a flourish, folded it neatly and sat down opposite her. There was no one else in the shop so she could finally relax.

She could see Anabella was trying to hold back tears.

"You're worrying me Anabella. What's got you so worked up. You can tell me."

"Yes, you do need to know."

Anabella dabbed at her teary eyes with a hanky plucked from her vintage black box purse, "I am afraid I got involved with a bad crowd in the penitentiary. They talked me into doing things I am not real proud of."

Raquel leaned forward and placed a reassuring hand on her shoulder. "Well, you just have to tell the police about it. It can't be that bad. You are not there anymore. You're a free agent now."

"That's just the problem!" she exclaimed. "They can get to you in the real world. You are still working for them, I mean. I may have to leave my home. I need to distance myself from this situation. I need to get away as far as possible."

"You make it sound serious."

Tears started to tumble down her powdered cheeks again, "It is, it is. They've followed me here. To Brumby Flat. There are things happening that I have no control over. And you need to be careful."

Raquel frowned and studied Anabella, "What do you mean by that?" she asked.

"I'm sorry. I know what happened to Mrs. Bette Mitchell. And they'll come after you as well."

"Me? Christ, Anabella. Now you really have to tell me everything. What's seriously going on?"

She sighed heavily and twisted the peace symbol necklace around between her fingers.

"There's no more hiding it. When I was in jail, I started to get these typed letters soon after I had arrived. From a secret admirer, or so it seemed. They knew everything about what had happened to me, and they were sympathetic. At first, I felt comforted by these letters I was receiving, and then the tone of the letters started to change. They took on a disturbing tone. It was like they wanted me to pursue a course of… revenge."

"And did you? You didn't, did you?"

Anabella shook her head, "Of course not. The language was very persuasive though. I've resisted it so far."

"Well, then I don't understand why you are so worried."

She clutched Raquel's arm, "I said no to them. These people, they don't accept no as an answer. There's people here in town that…"

She suddenly fell silent and rested back against the chair. She took a small compact out of her handbag and checked out her eye makeup.

"I think you need to talk to the police about your worries. Not me, Anabella. And if you know anything about Bette, it's really best to tell them. Have you still got those letters?"

She sniffed and put her damp hanky away back into her purse, "No, I tore them up. Perhaps you're right. I might have a quick chat to the police. Your son is a Police Officer, isn't he?"

"Yes."

"You know, I miss being a volunteer here in the Raindrops Shop. It was great fun, having Bette, Chris and that shy ex-librarian girl around. Gosh, I've completely forgotten her name. And baking for the customers," at this point, she stopped and glanced down at the floor, "I didn't mean for what happened. It was really an accident."

Raquel nodded, "I believe you, Anabella. Anyway, let's not go over the past again. Just do me a favour and see the police, as soon as you can."

She got to her feet and scooped up her purse, "Yes. I'd better be on my way. It's past lock up time. I didn't realise how late I was."

"It was lovely to see you again. Don't be a stranger."

Raquel followed her to the front door and latched it after

Anabella was out. She looked down at her watch and realised time was short to get her food shopping done. She quickly cleaned the counter benches and the coffee machine. Switching off the main lights, she locked the shop door firmly behind her.

Her car was parked in the front, on the street. She looked up and down the quiet main street, wondering why Phil Duncan had not dropped by all day. She was so used to him being on the charm offensive.

She decided not to dwell on the fact and drove off down the freeway, heading to the next town's supermarket. The sky was starting to slowly darken but the road ahead was clear. She put the car headlights on anyway.

She glanced back in the rear-view mirror briefly and noticed a small truck situated far behind. She looked at the road ahead again. Seconds later she glanced back in the mirror and this time, the truck seemed to have made up quite a lot of ground. She was going one hundred kilometres an hour and the truck had to be going much faster than the speed limit.

She thought what an idiot driver. Typical. No police around to book them for speeding.

She kept driving along until she felt a bump. At first, she thought she must have driven over a pothole in the road, but when she looked in the rear-view mirror, she saw the white truck's front bumper was right up to the rear of her car. The cabin of the truck was high so all she could see was the hands of the driver clutching the steering wheel.

She felt a distinctive second bump, shunting her car forward. She struggled to hold the car straight and keep it on the road.

"What the fuck!" she exclaimed aloud. She put her foot

down hard on the accelerator and surged ahead. She was clear of the truck for a short time, but it had also picked up speed.

Suddenly, a third bump came and this time, something went clunk and fell off her car. Raquel was certain it was part of the bumper bar.

She picked up speed again, but she knew it would not work. Her aggressor would just pick up speed and the vicious cycle would continue until she had crashed her car.

Raquel realised that she had nowhere safe to go. It wasn't safe to pull up alongside of the road. And she was still a good distance away from the next town. She did the only thing she could think of to do. She slowed down and set the car to veer between two leaning, badly damaged fence posts on the left, with the aim to hit the low barbed wire stretched across it. Possibly kangaroos had recently crashed through the fence. The wire easily snapped under the weight and force of her car and the Pontiac careened safely across the empty dry stretch of paddock. She had travelled over the hard ground and then through the bright yellow canola field for a good twenty metres before applying the brakes firmly. When she had successfully stopped her car, she glanced back over her left shoulder, to see what had happened to the white truck.

"Oh fuck," she gasped as she saw the truck had parked on the gravel verge of the freeway and a dark figure had emerged from the cabin. They were walking ominously across the paddock towards her. Their features were masked by the dark, stretched shadows cast by late afternoon.

Certain that the stranger was the killer of Bette Duncan, Raquel got out quickly, crab stepping over the waist-deep canola, she popped the boot lid open with some difficulty. She reached for a large bottle of water she had stashed in there and a small, lightweight blanket. She had placed her purse in her skirt side pocket and held her mobile phone in her trembling right hand along with her car key. She locked the car. Without looking behind her again, she crashed her way through the field of canola, heading for the trees on the hill. She had to put as much distance between herself and the mad truck driver. When she made it to the tree line, she raced over the dry ground cover of gum leaves and small twigs, pushing her way between spindly gum trees and shrubs. She ran for a good three minutes before stopping to catch her breath. Twigs and branches had torn some of her clothing, her lovely floral skirt the worst off with a frayed new hemline.

She looked nervously behind her. She wasn't sure if she was still being followed, but she decided it was best to keep moving forward. She brushed off the canola buds, leaves and twigs which had attached to the hem of her skirt. She kept on going, her heart racing inside her chest. She ran into thicker bushland and when she stopped for the second time, she noticed the sun was starting to slowly set in the sky. She leaned her back, which was wet from perspiration against the trunk of a large blue gum and dialled Duncan's mobile number. He answered after three rings.

"Phil."

"Hey, how are you?" he answered her brightly.

"Listen. I think I'm lost. I have no idea where I am right now, "she started to cry, and he finally sensed the panic in her voice.

"Slow down, slow down. Are you okay?"

"Phil. There was a guy trying to run me off the road. I drove into a paddock, and I just ran. I went into the bush. No idea where I am now."

"Where's the paddock, honey?"

"I was heading south on the freeway. I think…I drove the car off the road about twenty kilometres from Brumby Flat. I went through a fence into a canola field."

"It's okay. I'm with Detective Longmeil. You stay right where you are, don't lose your phone. Watch the battery. We'll drive and look for your car. Which way did you run?"

"I ran straight up the hill. Oh god. Hurry. It's starting to get dark."

"Are you safe where you are, Raquel?"

"Yeah, I think so. I think whoever it was, they're not chasing me anymore."

"Okay. Hang up now. Call me back immediately if something is wrong."

Raquel closed the call and slid down the tree trunk, trying to hold back her tears, which threatened to overwhelm her. She took a swig from the water bottle and bunched the small blanket over her knees and felt very alone. She was only comforted by the birds chirping and singing, high up in the trees. The singing would soon stop when darkness finally trickled its way across the landscape. She looked around at her strange surroundings and tried to work out which direction to walk. She knew Duncan or anyone else would never find her there, in the middle of the bush. Eventually she got up, dusted her knees and chose to walk north. She switched off the mobile for a while, to save the battery.

Chapter Sixteen

The flashing lights of the Ambulance and police cars lit up the surrounding bushland, making it twinkle like an outdoor Christmas display.

Raquel was sitting alone on the very edge of a park bench. She was fortunate to have stumbled onto the town's nature walking trail after spending hours walking around in complete darkness, with only a handful of stars to light her way.

The hem of her skirt had small rips, holes and tears from navigating the rough terrain and her feet were very sore from wearing ordinary dress shoes. She tripped in the darkness a few times, the worst was the tree root which also pulled her down and she banged her forehead on a neighbouring tree stump. She had a small lump there now but otherwise she was feeling alright.

The Ambos had draped a towel over her shoulders and given her the 'all clear' medically. They had also given her a cup of ice-cold water which she was sipping slowly to address her thirst. She felt lucky to be alive, having walked for hours in the bush. She was certain that she had walked around in circles for some time too, before stumbling onto the walking trail. She had to guess which way led back to town, but fortunately she had a good sense of direction. By the time she got to the last twenty metres of the trail, the police met her with flashlights on.

She looked up briefly now and saw the painted town silos were not far away. It made her think of Phil Proctor for a few moments. She wondered where he was and what he was doing. A part of her sorely missed his charm and charismatic easy smile. He had been, for the most part, a kind, caring man and attentive lover.

She glanced down the trail, and she could see a dark silhouette running towards the flashing lights, coming towards her.

She stood up shivering, her joints stiff from a cold night spent along the walking trail which stretched and twisted for kilometres through bushland. She clutched the corners of the towel across her chest. The figure became clearer to her as they rapidly approached. Finally, she could see who it was.

Duncan raced up to her, wearing what looked to be his best suit, shirt and tie. He opened his arms to her in a wide, welcoming arc. Teary eyed and overwhelmed with happiness to see him, someone she knew, she ran into his open embrace. He hugged her tight against his body. He was warm against her, and they were bathed in the added warmth of the flashing, brilliant lights dancing all around them.

"Oh my god, are you okay?" he breathed, removing his glasses with the sweep of one hand and slipping them into his navy jacket pocket. Then he held her again with both arms securely wrapped around her shoulders.

She nodded her head up and down, her hair brushing against his chest, "I'm just very cold. It was a bloody cold night. I walked for hours. I have some scratches, and see? A small bump on my head."

"That's okay. I'll warm you up," he kissed the top of her forehead, which surprised her, "I was so worried about you. I tried to call you back. I haven't been able to think, worrying about you."

"My phone went flat quickly."

"That explains it."

"I was chased, Phil. By some maniac driving a large white truck. Whoever it was, they tried to run me off the bloody freeway. They hit my car three times. It was crazy and so scary."

Duncan nodded, "Yeah, I know. I was with Detective Longmeil when you called me. We came looking for you, and we found your car abandoned. Just where you said, more or less. Is your son here too?"

"He's on his way, they said. He's off duty. Is my car okay?"

"I'm sure it is. It's been towed away. It didn't look too bad but I'm a detective, I'm not a mechanic."

He stood back slightly, his blue eyes intensely studying her face, and he entwined his fingers with hers. His touch made her shiver, and she believed there was a show of feeling somewhere in that touch. She found his attention was confusing her again, at a time when she was fully prepared to explore new possibilities.

"What is it?" she asked him, letting the towel finally slip off her shoulders.

"Well, I guess I am just happy to see that you're safe. I've been up all night. I was so worried. Did you tell the police everything that happened last night?"

She nodded, "Yes, but I didn't get the rego of the truck. It all happened so damn fast. And I didn't get to see the guy's face either. I don't know if they'll catch them, from what I told them. I didn't get much I guess because I was so bloody scared."

"Maybe you'd better stay with me and Longmeil, at my place, while they're still at large. Whoever they are, they tried to run you off the road. They've attempted to kill you tonight. They might try again."

"Phil, I don't think that's a good idea. To stay with you, I mean. It would be better if we stayed well away from each other. Don't you think? We don't want to complicate things."

He knitted his eyebrows together, "Why? It's easy. I'll just ask the department if we can protect you. We have to find who is responsible for the recent bashing of Templeton-Moore, my Bette's death and of course, what happened to Kitty."

"Phil, wait. I can't. Okay? I can't do this."

She had raised her voice. He stood firm, still looking puzzled.

"You need to be protected. Surely, you can see that."

"No, Phil. You married my best friend. And I don't want you to get the wrong idea about anything. I moved on, from us, a long time ago. We're just not supposed to be together. I'm sorry."

Her words sunk in. He let her fingers go, adrift and he pulled away. He then turned his back to take his leave of her.

"Well, okay, that's good. I am glad you're okay. Look after yourself. I'll still ask the department, if they need to set up surveillance for you."

"We're really good friends, aren't we?" she asked him nervously.

He turned his head back to study her. He revealed a

twisted half smile on his face which was difficult to read, "Of course, we are. Always, good friends."

As he walked away, she saw her son Steve running towards her.

"Raquel, are you okay?"

She opened up her arms and hugged her tall policeman son tight. She was relieved to be with him again.

"Yes I am. I'm pretty shaken up but I'm okay. I just hope they can catch the guy who tried to run me off the road."

"I told you to be careful."

"You only said to lock my door, honey."

****

He peered anxiously through the dusty, tattered cream lace curtains he had parted. He was standing in his dark, gloomy lounge room. His ashen grey, heavily lined face was more solemn than usual. He had his smudged reading glasses on, with the tiny crack in the left-hand corner so he peered over them to see into the distance.

Seventy-five-year-old John Templeton-Moore was a man clearly in a hurry. His son had warned him about the need to leave town as soon as possible, for reasons unknown. He did however notice how upset his son was, so he took the urgency of departure onboard. But before he could leave, he had to arrange to sell his home in town and quickly sign the sales agency agreement. He had called the new local real estate agent Sullivan O'Grady at least an hour ago and he was promised he would be there ten minutes earlier. Templeton-Moore glanced down at his wristwatch for the fifteenth time and cursed loudly. He didn't think much of late comers. He opened the fragile curtains even wider to see both ends of the street for any sign of activity.

After waiting a few more minutes, he let the fragile curtains fall together and the dust from them swirled into the air. He brushed his now dusty hands over his red flannel shirt which had seen better days and headed to his tiny and barely serviceable kitchen. He decided to make himself a quick cup of tea, while he was still waiting for the agent to appear. His old, well-worn trousers were beginning to fall down again, so he readjusted his belt one more notch as he filled up his old whistling kettle. He lit the flame for the gas stove and dragged an old wooden chair across the floor to sit at the laminate table. He waited impatiently for the kettle to boil and the agent to turn up.

His hearing wasn't all the best, but he turned his head when he thought he heard a knocking at his front door. He took the kettle off the boil, cursed to himself again and rushed into the hallway. He opened the door to the street and only the flush of a warm breeze forced its way inside.

Suddenly, he heard another sound coming from his kitchen, which had to be his screen door slamming against the door frame. He inadvertently left the front door ajar and headed back to the kitchen.

"Hey mate. Why didn't you bloody use the front door, like normal people do?" He bellowed out, believing it was Sullivan O'Grady. He entered his kitchen and found no one was there. Except the back screen door was swinging in the breeze and sometimes connecting with a bang against the door frame.

He sighed and returned the whistling kettle to the stove.

A floorboard creaked behind him, and before he had the

time to turn his head and react, he fell to his knees when the blow came. His cheap reading glasses cluttered across the hard floor and snapped in two.

He moaned and felt the top of his head. His trembling right hand came away with his blood. He tried to get up and turn to look at his attacker, but he then felt a force drag him by the collar of his flannel shirt. They dragged him backwards, across the kitchen floor. He made a frantic grab for a table leg in a vain attempt to save himself.

Winded by his desperate efforts, with the shirt neckline cutting into this throat and windpipe, he struggled to call out for help. His arms failed out and upset a number of items lining the kitchen island bench, including a full knife block and the toaster oven. They cluttered against the floor and the knifes scattered across it. His assailant dug their knee on top of his chest and with one of the strewn knives drawn, slashed away at his throat. They made the intended target, blood trickled down his neck and then Templeton-Moore's face was pushed into the floor. He was trying to cry out again.

"Shut up! Shut up!" a strange voice was growling the words into his left ear.

Templeton-Moore tried to desperately reach for one of the fallen knives but couldn't quite grasp it. His fingers just brushed the silver handle when the unimaginable happened.

His assailant lashed out again, this time the large knife was raised high and savagely came down on Templeton-Moore's' right hand. Three of his fingers were severed through. Templeton-Moore tried to scream but blood just bubbled and gurgled from the two-inch angry gash straight across his throat.

"Your bloody son didn't obey his instructions, did he," the

strangers' taunting voice hissed close to his ear again.

Templeton-Moore could not see the face of his attacker, but he did see the shadow of a knife raised again, ready to inflict more damage. He tried to struggle and break free.

Suddenly, a voice rang out from somewhere in the house. "Hello? John?"

The assailant fell quiet and stood motionless over his maimed victim.

Then a floorboard creaked, and the same voice called out, "John? It's me, Sullivan."

The uncomfortable silence continued.

Sullivan yelled out again from the hallway, "It's Sullivan, and I bought someone else along with me."

The assailant made the snap decision to quickly leave the premises. He had no intention to confront other people. He removed his knee from his victims' chest, rose awkwardly and raced out the back screen door, still holding the bloodied knife in hand. The screen door swung back and forth on its rusted hinges as his victim screamed.

It was at this precise moment that Sullivan entered the kitchen and found John Templeton-Moore prostrate on the kitchen floor, trying to desperately breathe after his exertion, with his head lying in a small but growing pool of blood.

****

Detective Longmeil exchanged meaningful glances with Constable Willaston before they sat down in front of O'Grady. Longmeil was not accustomed to taking the lead in a murder investigation but with Phillip Duncan presently off the case, he had to step up and take charge. Fortunately, young Willaston was happy to obey all instructions.

If O'Grady was nervous, he certainly didn't show it. He was seated calmly on the other side of the Constable's desk at the local police station. He smoothed his perfect curled sandy hair back with his long fingers and played with his cigarette packet in his other hand.

"You know why you're here, don't you?" Longmeil started, with a dash of sarcasm in his voice.

Sullivan twisted his neck, "No. I have no idea, mate. I gave you people my statement yesterday."

"You can't smoke in here."

Sullivan put the cigarettes away with some reluctance. "It's okay. I had no intention to. Just thinking when we're done, I can have one. Okay, so what's up? What more can I do for you?"

Longmeil leaned forward, clasping his hands together on the desk, "I have called you in, to understand what exactly happened to John Templeton-Moore."

Sullivan smirked, folded his arms and leaned back in his chair, "I explained it the other day. I don't know why you want me to repeat me self. Why don't you spit it out, what's really bothering you?"

"According to your statement, you didn't see his attacker."

"That's right, Detective Longmeil. By the time I made it to the kitchen, I reckon they had left through the back door. I remember the screen door was kind of moving, swinging. Like someone had left in a hurry, you know."

"You were the only one there at the house, and you found him on the floor."

He nodded, "Yeah, I did. The poor guy was really messed up. In a bad way. I called an ambulance straight away."

"Well, I suppose you did. But how do we know that? How do we know that your version of events is the correct one? You were alone with Templeton-Moore in the house. No one else saw you, or apparently, the intruder go inside the house."

Sullivan started to look ruffled. He straightened up in the office chair and coughed to clear his suddenly parched dry throat.

"Good god, mate. I'm not the person you're looking for. I didn't kill anyone, and I didn't do anything to John. I found him in a bad way. I had an appointment to meet him at his house because he wanted to sell it. That's way I was there in the first place. I had the sales agency form ready to go."

Constable Willaston spoke up, "Yes, that's true. I searched his car."

Longmeil shot him an impatient, icy glance, "I know, I know. But the fact remains. Sullivan, you have no good alibi for the wedding, or the night when Bette Duncan was killed. And on top of it, yourself and John Templeton-Moore were the only ones who witnessed what happened in his home the other day."

O'Grady looked blank at the desk in front of him, his attractive velvety brown eyes open wide.

"And the trouble is, John can't talk about it unfortunately. He is not only traumatised by the assault, but his throat is damaged, and his right hand is now useless. Can't write. Can't talk."

"Yeah, so?"

"I know more about your family."

O'Grady leaned forward in his chair, "Hang on. Excuse

me. What's my bloody family got to do with this?"

"I'm very glad you asked. It's more than a rumour in town. I have it on good authority that your family and the Templeton-Moore family have had a disagreement over a parcel of land for decades. As you're both neighbours, you can't keep a feud like that quiet. So, it would not be surprising to me, if you seized your chance to get back at John's family. Any outsider would assume the same thing. You were alone O'Grady, right there in John's house. Under his roof. And why not take the opportunity to change your family's fortune?"

O'Grady's large brown eyes glazed over.

"I think that's a crappy, shitty assumption to make," he retorted.

Longmeil smirked. He knew he had O'Grady squirming in his chair.

He continued, "I can't match up the rest of this mess to you. The model and Bette Duncan. But I'm certain that you tortured John. You had the motive, and you had the opportunity. Isn't it time for you to 'fess up to it?"

Sullivan O'Grady shook his head and leant back in the chair, "Okay mate. You win. I'm going to have to call my lawyer in. We're done, mate."

Chapter Seventeen

Anabella Williams was seated elegantly in her time capsule nineteen-fifties living room, reading a vintage nineteen-sixties pulp fiction crime novella. She glanced up at her parents' old cuckoo clock and noticed it was four-thirty in the afternoon. Even when she wasn't going out all day, she still put on her best vintage clothes, teased her hair up and applied her make up. She was wearing a lined white crochet shift dress, with cream ankle boots and a gravity defying beehive hairdo. She popped up her head over the book pages when she heard a loud persistent knocking on her front door.

She uncurled her long legs and rested the book in the shape of a steeple over the glass coffee table to keep her place. She patted a stray grey whisp of hair back into place before she opened the door to whoever it was.

Principal Reece Haddock stood there on her doorstep, wearing a three-piece brown suit, presenting a handgun pointed at her, for her viewing only. His hazel eyes were narrowed and serious. It was hard for her to read his facial expression behind his red tinged beard.

She gasped and raised her thinly pencilled eyebrows at him.

"Please, not a word to be said. Just back up slowly, thank

you," he said in a low, commanding voice.

She respectfully followed his instructions, and carefully backed down the hallway, careful not to lose her footing in her high heel boots. He followed her inside, lifting his gun higher.

"Who are you? What do you want with me?"

"You knew that I would have to turn up one day. I think it's time to tie up some loose ends, Mrs. Williams."

"It's you. Your voice. I know your voice. You are that man who keeps calling me!" she exclaimed, pointing her manicured forefinger at him.

"Yes, well. I do need to tie up some loose ends."

"Please, I won't say anything about this. You're not going to harm me, are you?"

"No. Not at the moment. But I do want you to call up your lovely friend, the Willaston woman in the shop. Ask her to come over now."

"She's going to ask me why," she said, her hands visibly shaking at her sides.

"Say it's important, that should do the trick."

He indicated her to move into the lounge room. She turned her back on him and walked forward. She slowly claimed her mobile phone from the dining room table. She was careful not to make any quick movements in front of him.

She dialled up the number and he added, "Put the call on loudspeaker."

She nodded and placed the mobile phone in mid-air between them. Her hand was noticeably trembling.

"Hi, Raquel, are you busy today?"

"Anabella?"

"Yeah. It's me. Hello, look, I need to see you right away.

Right now."

Reece stepped up and Anabella felt the gun nudging her ribs as she spoke.

"What's up?"

"I just need to see you. It's really very important. Meet me here at my house. Please, please. Come as soon as you can. Okay dear. Bye."

She hung up the call and Haddock quickly snatched the mobile phone out of her hand.

"That was very nicely done. Now, we sit. We wait."

Meanwhile, Raquel stood alone in her kitchen, thinking about what had just transpired. She was going to leave for Anabella's house right away, but something was telling her to hesitate. Instinctively, she called Phil Duncan.

"Okay hello Raquel, what can I help you with?" He replied lazily on the other end.

"Phil, Anabella Williams just called me. Her voice was strange sounding. She wants me to urgently come over to her place. I thought you might want to know."

"Is she having a tea party? Do you think I care?"

She took a sharp intake of breath and flicked her eyes to the ceiling, "Yes, I believe you do. I think you should meet me there. It's just a stab in the dark but she must know who the killer is. You didn't hear her voice, but I did. Maybe you'll have the information you need to make an arrest."

"I wish you won't use terms like 'stab in the dark'. Didn't you read today's paper or hear the radio? They've arrested Sullivan O'Grady, you know."

"Yeah, honestly. He's not the killer. Do you really believe that rubbish? Anabella's been hiding something since she came back to town."

There was a brief silence.

"Okay, okay. I'll meet you there, at her house. I'll be over there as soon as I can. Got to stop for some petrol first."

"I'll see you at her place. Please Phil. Please meet me there."

She closed the call. She wasn't happy with his half-hearted response. She knew that he wasn't a fan of rejection and she had let him down several times already. But she hoped he would see past it and realise what was important. Finding Bette's killer.

She rushed out to her car and drove straight to Anabella's house.

Stepping out of the car, Raquel immediately noticed the front door was wide open, which was unusual. She looked around the garden and up the driveway, in case Anabella was bending over, working away at weed eradication in the garden. The weeds were taller than her flower beds.

"Hello? Anabella, I'm here," she yelled out, into the shadows of the hallway. The hall light was off, and she couldn't see too far.

No answer came.

She advanced forward, unsure what to do or say next. As her foot touched tentatively down on the floorboards, Reece appeared from the shadows, one hand clasping Anabella's arm in a vice like grip and dragging her along with him. She winched in pain.

"Well, good to see you've made it, Miss Willaston. Come here and join your good friend Anabella," he said with a smirk, waving the gun at her.

Raquel froze and stiffened her back, "What do you want, Reece?" she asked him quietly, trying hard not to show fear.

"I wanted to…explain everything to you. I know you're close to that detective. Someone needs to know the burden of my truth."

"Okay. Go on. I'm listening."

He indicated for Raquel and Anabella both to sit down on her family's club lounge.

"I know Bette Duncan told you everything. She saw that photo in my office. She did, didn't she?"

She nodded, "The one with you and her old friend Mandy-Jane? Yeah, she noticed it. She told me."

"Well, Mandy-Jane Fischer was a beautiful girl. Not an academically brilliant student, mind you but she had other admirable qualities. You could say that I fell under her spell. She was a bewitching young lady, older than her friends. As a teacher, you have to remain distant from your students. Unfortunately, I crossed the line. I fell quite heavily for Mandy-Jane. I was her secret lover. But it lasted a short time only. A great love affair almost always fizzles out, soon after it's exploded."

"You're not seriously saying…"

He cut her off, "Yes, we met in secret after school. Had to be after school. Being with a student, well, that would've been the end of my great teaching ambitions you know. However, I had a clever way around the situation."

"Do I really need to know about this?" Raquel asked, but he angrily waved his gun at her face and she flinched.

"Yes, you do. I asked my brother Mitch to help me, so he picked her up from school. But that soon became a problem unfortunately."

Haddock took a deep breath before continuing, "He was younger than me, my brother. He very unfortunately fell for

Mandy-Jane too. So, the pair of them met in secret too, behind my back. He would pick her up from school, and I don't know where they went, but they had some fun together. Can you imagine…how I felt? I was her supposed legitimate lover."

He lapsed into silence and Raquel noticed his gun was lowered a fraction. She dared to ask the question that needed to be asked.

"So, Reece. What really happened to Mandy-Jane?"

"At last, the million-dollar question is asked. It was a tragic accident, Miss Willaston."

Reece Haddock recalled the details for her.

****

At just twenty-four years old, Reece Haddock was a young maths and sciences teacher, and he had no shortage of teenage schoolgirls with racing hormones and heaving bosoms fawning over him and trying desperately to get his attention. Back then, he had shoulder length brown hair with a pleasing kink to it, a perfectly formed goatee and he wore well fitted suits. It was hard to ignore the teenage girls, but he had successfully navigated the mine field of their wild romantic imaginings until the day when Mandy-Jane Fischer confidently approached him.

He was assigned detention duty one rainy afternoon in June. She was kept back for detention for missing two art classes without a good excuse. As punishment, he had instructed her to read a poem out loud. She read Edgar Allan Poe like no one had read it to him before. She added actions and a high sense of drama to the narrative. She twirled in front of him, lying across tabletops in her short school dress, stretching her body against the blackboard and dropping to her knees to die a dramatic death. Reece finally yielded to temptation. At the end of her arousing performance, he put out his hands to help her up and planted a brief kiss firmly on her lips. To his surprise, she kissed him back with passion, and as he found out later, she was completely open to all his erotic experiments and darkest thoughts. They were very adventurous with their intimacy.

It was an intense affair doomed to end badly.

One day, his brother Mitch had picked Mandy-Jane up as usual.

Reece Haddock had arrived home to his inner-city apartment a bit later than expected. He had been asked to attend a teachers' meeting in relation to a planned Easter excursion for the year eleven boys. The meeting ran one hour over, so by the time it finished, he glanced down at his watch and noticed it was past five o'clock. He left in haste, nearly bowling over Principal Sheppard who grunted, "Hey, excuse me."

Reece mumbled an apology and bolted out the door. He drove home on auto pilot.

He parked his car quickly on the street and burst through his front door. He entered straight into his small open lounge and kitchen area, and it didn't take him long to realise something about the scene was amiss.

He walked in to find Mandy-Jane and his younger brother Mitch seated on his couch together. She was twirling a lock of her hair and her knees were raised with her bare feet up on the seat. His brother was seated on the opposite end, his left arm cradled over the generous arm rest. Their rigid look and the uncomfortable silence which hung in the air had Reece's mind racing. He was entertaining the thought that they had been fooling around before he arrived. As he walked up to Mandy-Jane, he noticed much more than he bargained for or wanted to know. Her lipstick was slightly smudged, as was her eye makeup and the hem of her short school uniform was caught up on the frilly edge of her knickers. She was usually very neat and tidy. When he looked into her eyes, she looked away after a couple of seconds and he saw her swallow hard against her velvet neck choker.

He stood over them, noticing Mitch fidgeting, rubbing his hands.

"Thanks for bringing her by," he said to his brother. He slapped his shoulder.

Mitch nodded, "That's okay. Let me know when I have to drop her off," he got off the couch, thrust his hands in his jeans' pockets and quietly closed the front door behind him.

When they were alone, Reece studied her more closely, "How are you? How was your day at school?"

He stepped forward, bending over to kiss her, but she evaded him and slid across onto the other end of the couch.

"You are *not* my father. For Christ's sake," she snapped at him, "You're like my old man when you wanna be."

She got up and turned her back on him. It was uncharacteristic of her to be so cold towards him.

"Okay. I get it now. Sorry I'm late. I had a teachers' meeting…and it ran overtime."

She shook out her punk style light brown hair and stretched, "Don't know why you bothered to bring me here and see me at all. I could be home with my family right now, having dinner."

Reece stepped forward and placed his hand softly on her

right shoulder, "Don't do this. I said I was sorry. Come on MJ, I don't want to fight with you. I'd rather make out."

She turned to face him, her pale blue eyes shining bright, "Reece. No. We can't go on this way. You might as well know the truth. Mitch said not to say anything, but I will. I think I am in love with your brother."

Reece raised his eyebrows and started to laugh heartily, "With Mitch? You're in love with Mitch? He's just a young lad."

"Look Reece. You need to get it. You need to understand."

"What is it, that I have to understand, MJ?"

"Mitch. He's more my age. We've been spending some time together. You only have yourself to blame for it. You threw us together."

He began pacing around her, brushing his fingers through his mane of hair. He was struggling to understand what she was telling him.

"MJ, I thought we had a strong connection," he said in a voice of despair mixed with shock.

"We do, but I really like Mitch. I'm sorry but it just kind of happened. We didn't plan it this way. I'll always enjoy what we had Reece, but it's over. I've made up my mind who I want to be with."

He looked at her in a way that he had not looked at her before, and she shivered,

"Fuck no. That's not right. You can't just leave me," he said very quietly, in a low tone of voice.

"I can do whatever I want. You do not own me. Call Mitch, I wanna go home right now."

Something snapped inside of Reece. His face turned a

bright beetroot red, and he exploded into a fit of rage.

He lunged forward, grabbed Mandy-Jane by her pale throat and pushed her backwards hard onto his couch. She was completely taken by surprise by his aggression, and she fell backwards like a discarded toy. His body quickly covered hers and he grabbed her wrists with one hand in a vice like grip. With his left hand, he covered her nose and mouth and pressed down hard. She tried hard to scream, her blue eyes wide with terror, but Reece seemed to hold her down with an almost superhuman strength. She wriggled her body, trying frantically to break free of his crushing weight. She was struggling to breathe. The force of his hand disfigured her nose, pushing it flat and he watched her frightened eyes change.

Her eyes eventually rolled back into her head as she passed out and then, a minute later her body went completely limp. He could feel there was no more resistance.

Reece finally let go his left hand and sat back on the couch. He covered his own mouth and started to sob uncontrollably. He now understood what he had done.

He stared down at Mandy-Jane who was lying so very still on the couch, her left arm touching the floor limply with her partially closed eyes staring up at the ceiling. Her hair was dishevelled with whisps plastered across her cheeks and forehead from the sweat of his exertion, and her slender long legs were barely covered by her school uniform. She no longer could talk, move or think. Her earthly connection was completely gone.

Reece felt waves of nauseousness suddenly overcome him and he raced to the bathroom. He was sick for a while, before he composed himself well enough to come back and take a long hard look at his Mandy-Jane.

He was secretly hoping she was about to wake up. She looked like she was in a deep sleep, and he was sure he could still see her chest breathing. But it was not to be. He sat rigidly next to her lifeless body for another ten minutes before calling his brother.

"Hey Mitch. I've done something stupid. Better come back now."

Mitch had his own key to Reece's apartment, and he opened the front door. He found Reece bent over, his head in his hands and Mandy-Jane lying listless beside him. His eyes teared up and shock set in.

"Oh my god, oh my god," he spun around, lifting his hands up into the air,

"She's not dead, she's not dead…she's bloody dead, isn't she?" he exclaimed.

Reece got up, his hands embracing his arms and shook him gently, "Be quiet. Please. Be quiet. I need to think what to do about this. It was an accident."

"Man, you have to call the police, we have to do the right thing."

Reece spun around angrily.

"No, Mitch. Do you know what's going to happen to me? I'll go straight to bloody jail. My career, my life will be rooted. It was a tragic accident. I just need some time to think what to do."

Mitch sat down on the very edge of the couch, staring helplessly at Mandy-Jane. His hands were visibly shaking.

"We'll have to take her somewhere. Dump her body," Reece said calmly, as he paced the floor.

"Reece. I'm not doing it. Not helping you," his brother got up to leave, but Reece cut off his exit.

"Hey, you're my family. We're mates. We're brothers, you and I. We help each other out."

They spent the next few hours arguing in low voices and eventually planning what to do. They waited until it was dark to make their move. Mitch backed his car down the driveway and in pitch black darkness, they carried her body to the boot. In the dark, it looked like they were carrying a couple of large canvas bags between them.

As they drove far away from Reece's inner-city apartment, they made a lasting secret pact between them. It remained unbroken and unspoken of up to the time of Mitch's tragic death in a motorcycle accident five years later.

They drove and parked near a well-known reservoir. Reece knew where there was a broken line of fence. All the local kids knew about it.

They struggled with her body through it and finally at the water's edge, they unravelled her body from its canvas prison. Before they had removed her body from the apartment, they had been careful to clean her naked body of any evidence of foul play and of any evidence. Her stiff, naked body slipped into the water, making the smallest of ripples and she floated away from them, pretty face down. They crept quietly away, unnoticed.

Over a week later when her body was discovered, an act of suicide was soon ruled out. By then, Reece Haddock had completely composed himself. While the media reported a daily tirade of half-truths and his school went to pieces for losing one of their own, he went under the radar. Her family grieved and asked for the public's help to catch her killer. He was never suspected. He was never formally questioned by the police.

****

Standing in Anabella's lounge room, Reece Haddock completed his story.

"I knew she was fooling around with my brother by then, and I was a bit rougher than usual with her. I started to strangle her and I found…I could not stop myself from doing it. Then I held my hand over her mouth and nose. She couldn't breathe and I just let her die right there. She pleaded to me with her eyes. But I couldn't stop myself. After, I rang Mitch and we had to work out what to do with her body."

"Oh my god." Anabella gasped, and dabbed a hanky under her eyes.

"Mitch was beside himself. I destroyed our mateship, you know. Completely."

He looked down at the floor and the gun in his hand lowered again. Raquel straightened her back, and her legs were ready to spring into action. Her mind was racing, trying to work out a means of escape. She gently nudged Anabella and flicked her eyes to Haddock's deep in thought stance so she could see what was happening. Haddock nearly looked remorseful. Suddenly, she was forced to stop thinking about escape as he snapped back from the burden of his memories. The gun was raised again to his chest height, directed at the two women.

"We drove up to the reservoir late in the night and dumped her body in the water. We agreed not to talk about her ever again. It was easy to get away with it. No one interviewed either of us. No one knew who Mandy-Jane was seeing. No one else had cared enough. But I cared for her deeply. I didn't plan to kill her. It just happened, and I couldn't stop myself from…" his voice trailed off, "I went on with my life, my career, but I thought about her every day. Honestly, I did. I have suffered."

Raquel simply nodded and the gesture seemed to calm Reece.

"Sometimes, I nearly forgot what I did. I start to believe it was an accident. That she really drowned; you know? Then I remember. It comes screaming back into my head. She won't go away."

He was suddenly interrupted by a sound out in the hallway. He sprang into action, his gun raised ominously again as he peered around the corner.

Duncan had just walked in, unaware of the danger he was about to face and he yelled out Anabella's name in the entrance hall.

"Stop where you are," Reece yelled out, watching the ladies with one eye and waving the gun squarely at Duncan's chest, "Drop your gun, Detective. Now. On the floor."

"It's okay, Reece. Relax. I'm not armed. I'm unarmed."

Duncan carefully raised both his hands above his shoulders and was immediately ushered into the lounge room to join the ladies. Raquel tried to meet his gaze to find out if he had a gun. Duncan slightly shook his head before he sat down, and she immediately understood.

"Why did you come here?" Reece wildly waved his gun at his chest.

"I was just passing by," he lied, trying to sound calm and keep his breathing steady.

"Well, this is very awkward for me. I had plans for two, not three of you."

Duncan finally sat down, squeezing himself between Anabella and Raquel on the wide club lounge. He positioned himself there, in his mind to protect the women if Reece made his murderous move. He lowered his arms.

"Now that you are here, Detective, I am not going to repeat my story."

Duncan smirked and carefully raised his right hand to adjust his glasses on his nose, "That's okay by me. I have a feeling I may know some of it anyway. It's about three good friends at high school. Teenage girls. But I'd prefer to know what's your plan now?"

"I don't honestly know what to do. I need time to think about it."

"Did you kill my wife?" Duncan asked him quietly, point blank.

Reece looked uncomfortable. He advanced forward and the barrel of his gun dug into Duncan's left cheek. Duncan closed his eyes and braced himself for the worst. The intensity of the change of mood, made Raquel turn her head slightly and she let out a surprised gasp. Anabella just stared straight ahead.

"Not directly, Detective."

Raquel could see Duncan's cheeks going red with inner rage.

"Yes, I'd better explain why I said that. I paid for someone else to do it. I have friends in low places, you might say, who are in desperate need of cash funds. He didn't hesitate to do the deed for me."

Duncan tried to get up, but Raquel had looped her arm

through his and firmly held on. She held him down.

"I am sorry, but your wife knew too much. And if she didn't know, it wasn't going to take her long to figure it out. It was stupid of me to put that photo up on my office wall. Too late now. I should've known better. I was inviting trouble in."

"Reece. You're a vile creature. A blight on this Earth," Duncan said through his gritted teeth, "People in town will notice our disappearance."

"Sshhh, no," Raquel implored him to stay quiet, fearing for their lives.

"Very poetic. You've got a perfect right to your opinion, Detective. I'm not a pleasant fellow."

The gun barrel was withdrawn from Duncan's cheek. Reece stepped back and started to wave the gun around, pointing it menacingly and randomly at each one of them. At this, Anabella started to sob big splashy tears, Raquel shivered, and Duncan sat up straighter.

"So, who's going first?" he smiled in a teasing manner at their tense expressions. He walked up and down, a hand running through his hair.

"Just having a bit of fun. Yes. It's a big problem I have now, having the three of you here. I wonder if someone else will turn up on the doorstep. I have been haunted, but not actually hunted. It's been a very privileged life really."

He suddenly lowered the gun, left them seated in the loungeroom as he strode confidently into Anabella's kitchen. A single shot rang out, reverberating throughout the house and then there was an enormous thud against the lino tiled floor.

Duncan was the first to move. He leapt to his feet and

turning to the women, he said, "Okay. Stay right here."

Anabella screamed hysterically, lunging forward, but Raquel grabbed her waist and held her tight.

"No, don't go in there, Anabella."

Duncan investigated the kitchen on his own, to be confronted with Reece Haddock's still body and the remains of his head and blood splattered everywhere on the bamboo wallpapered walls and against the pale blue kitchen cupboards. He came back into the lounge room, wiping his eyeglasses on his clean shirt sleeve.

"It's okay. We're safe now. He's gone. I'll call it in."

"As in, he's dead?" Raquel piped up to which he just inclined his head.

Anabella kept on sobbing. Through her barrage of tears, she cried out, "I can't stay here anymore, not in this house. He's killed himself in my lovely kitchen. In our house."

She wailed out the last words and was barely audible after.

The Last Leg...

Detective Longmeil was leaning his full weight against Constable Banner's desk. He and Senior Detective Phillip Duncan were discussing closure notes of the case in the local police station. Duncan was seated comfortably in Constable Willaston's office chair, attired in his best tan trousers and fine pinstripe shirt.

"Well, it's over. Another Brumby bloody Flat murder fiasco behind us," he commented, taking out his notebook and scribbling some notes only he could decipher.

Longmeil nodded, cracked his knuckles and sighed deeply.

"Yeah, I'll be glad to stay in Adelaide for a bit. Did I tell you that my wife's threatening to divorce me? Man. I can't afford that to happen. We've got a lovely big house, live in an expensive suburb and the kids are in private school. But I really like the house."

"Sorry to hear that, mate."

"Oh well. It is what it is. Anyway, Reece Haddock did himself in. Lucky for you and the ladies."

Duncan heaved a sigh, leaned forward and rested his hands in a steeple position on Willaston's super tidy desk, "It was a close call. I thought he was actually going to kill us. He baited us for a while. It was a strange thing that happened. He very calmly walked into that kitchen and blew his bloody brains out."

Longmeil raised an eyebrow and shook his head, "Wow," he said, "I wonder why he hesitated."

"Look. He had blood on his hands already, and I guess the thought of dealing with three of us, it might've got to him. He knew if he killed us, his days of innocence was gone. His career would be over. He wasn't going to get away with it this time. It must've been years of living with regret for killing the schoolgirl he so adored," he said in a quiet tone, adding reflectively, "If you adore someone, you certainly don't kill them."

"I don't understand why he came out here, to work as a school Principal in Brumby Flat? It's like he wanted to be caught out."

"No. Maybe. He came looking for my Bette, I reckon. Too much of a coincidence when you think about it. I mean, he must've heard about our wedding and worked out that her old schoolfriend Kitty Caulfield would be here for it. He hoped maybe. It really explains how Kitty said she felt very comfortable with her attacker during our wedding reception. She knew him from high school. She trusted him. I guess he thought it was best to silence her as well. However, Willaston said he didn't confess to it. At any rate, Kitty still can't remember who her attacker was, and she's gone back to Sydney. Apparently, her modelling career has just skyrocketed. She's advertising some big mattress company and she's also the face of a new line of fancy bed sheets."

Longmeil stretched his long legs out, "Yeah, that makes total sense."

"And Williams said Reece kept saying something about tying up loose ends."

"I see."

"I feel sorry for poor old John Templeton-Moore. He's a lucky man to still be alive. That was our man Reece again. Templeton-Moore will never recover one hundred percent. Can't talk, can't write. Templeton-Moore's son coming from jail had the right qualifications to kill my Bette, with his truck licence. When he refused to finish off Raquel Willaston, Reece was forced to show his hand and threatened to kill his dear old man. Came close to succeeding too."

"Well, Ross Templeton-Moore is safely locked away. Don't know how long he'll be in jail for this time."

Duncan sniffed and shifted his weight in the chair, "That little bastard can stay there forever, as far as I'm concerned."

Longmeil looked down at the floor and said, "I'm sorry about your wife."

Duncan said nothing.

"On a different subject, Constable Willaston did a pretty good job with all his witness interviews and statements."

"Yeah, not too bad, but he's got to learn to focus on his job. The love distractions need to be under control."

"Love distractions?" Longmeil looked genuinely puzzled.

"Never mind. It's just an observation."

They lapsed into silence before Detective Longmeil interjected, "You know, I actually feel sorry for Mrs. Anabella Williams."

Duncan waved his right hand dismissively, "Look, I don't care. She was found to be conspiring with Reece. She was talking to him about taking revenge for what happened two years ago. She's not Miss squeaky clean Miss goody two shoes. She should've learnt her lesson and known better."

"But giving the old bird a two-year sentence? She didn't kill anyone. Not this time around."

"I *said* I don't feel the least bit sorry for her."

"Are you heading back to Adelaide too?" Longmeil asked, changing the subject.

Duncan shook his head, "No. I live in Brumby Flat now. I've got some important matters to sort out first. And there's also some unfinished business I have. In fact, I am on my way now to deal with it. Just wish me luck. Would you?"

He propelled himself out of the chair. He patted Longmeil's right arm and winked, as he walked past and left through the stations side door.

****

Duncan knocked soundly on her front door. He had to knock a couple more times before he could hear the sounds of movement within the house. He then forced his way inside when Raquel opened it a fraction to see who it was.

He grabbed her waist roughly. She knitted her eyebrows together, studying him closely.

"What are you doing? Have you gone crazy?" she exclaimed, backing away and trying to escape.

But he held her waist in a tight, vice like grip with both hands. She gasped and could feel his heart beating hard and quickly under her right palm. She breathed him in and felt quite giddy. She wondered if he had gone completely mad. She put her arms up in defence, trying to push him away.

"I know we haven't had," he said in his strong deep voice, then paused, "the best start and a lot of bumps along the road, on top of it. But the fact is, I kept thinking about you, Raquel, as much as I have tried very hard to forget. You started seeing Phil Proctor and I respectfully backed off."

"Okay," she half whispered. She started to relax a little in his grip.

"Yeah, and then I had a chance to see a future with Bette. We had a lot of great moments together. So, we got married."

"Hey, it's okay Phil. I know how the rest of this story goes. If this little talk of yours hasn't got a good ending to it, I don't want to hear about it anymore. I don't want to be upset, okay?"

He smirked but went on, "I miss Bette every day. Honestly, she's still there, inside my head. But you've always been there, these last few years. You have stood by me too. As frustrating and bloody infuriating as our relationship, or non-relationship has been, I am a free man now. I have to know. What about you and Proctor? Is there any hope left for you two to be together? I need to know. I need to know right now."

Raquel lowered her eyes, "Oh yes, we are well and truly finished. He's gone back to the states with his old man. He left last week. He hasn't contacted me or anything, so it's over. But I am dealing with it."

"Good. Good," he nodded his head and brushed his fingers lightly under her chin and his very touch felt sensual to her, "I am not promising that I'll make an honest woman of you. I am not offering you the moon or the stars, Raquel. But I would like us to be together. See how it goes. Move in with me, Raquel. I live in this big, lonely house now. I've got everything, but I haven't got you."

"How scandalous, Detective Duncan," she mused.

He grinned right back.

"No. Not in this bloody small town, nothing is too scandalous."

He leant forward, his breath blowing hot on her cheeks and then he slowly kissed her mouth and lingered there to kiss her softly again. He still held her waist and with his other hand, he held her face up. She felt his groin getting hot and she whimpered as he pressed himself greedily against her body. His hard on was plainly obvious.

He stopped for a moment, looking deep into her hazel eyes, "Come on. Let's begin all over again. Is it my place or yours?"

"Your place, for sure. But not now, please stay here tonight. I will accept your kind offer, Phil."

He grinned and he held her that bit tighter. And she gave herself completely to him, her body, heart and soul right then.

She lifted her T-shirt over her head, her blond hair spraying over her shoulders. She was braless and Duncan's eyes lingered on her erect nipples and pendulum breasts. He unbuttoned his white shirt to reveal his well-formed chest. He struggled out of the shirt sleeves and tenderly clasped her naked sides.

"How far away is your bedroom again?" he asked her, coming in closer, kneading his crotch against hers.

She inclined her head to the right.

"That far," he murmured, stroking her face and gently touching her breasts with his finger tips, teasing her.

He kissed her with abandon and passion. Gradually they shed the rest of their clothing piece by piece onto the living room floor, until they were completely naked. Still kissing feverishly and entwined in a hot embrace, they manoeuvred their way into her bedroom and fell onto her four-poster bed. He lay beneath her.

"How about those circus manoeuvres you know so well?" he whispered the words deeply into her left ear, before flicking his warm tongue inside.

She gave him a shy half smile. Then she effortlessly grabbed the top wooden frame of her four-poster bed and swung herself up. She balanced and stretched her naked body out and slipped effortlessly down, around the bedpost to straddle his hips. He patiently manoeuvred and lifted her hips slightly and slipped his firm hard cock inside of her. She gasped and moaned and tossed her head back as it touched her senses in all her pleasurable places.

Suddenly, Duncan burst into song, singing an Operatic aria and he made it sound so authentic that Raquel stared down at him in wide eyed wonder.

"What *are* you doing?" she exclaimed.

He paused for a brief moment of reflection, "I haven't sung to anyone before. Just feel like singing. Used to like Opera, you know?"

"You're such a Dag," she mused.

He grinned and started his aria again, enjoying her grinding up and down on his hard cock. He continued to sing to her until he exploded his load inside her and she arched her back as she came fast, soon after him.

He slapped her playfully on her behind and rolled over on top of her. Her chest was heaving, her nipples pricked like spikes against his sweat beaded chest.

"Do you think we're done? No. We have far more games to play," he whispered to her, flickering his pointy tongue in her left ear. He entwined his fingers with hers, as her hands lay palms up on the bed, above her shoulders and then deeply thrust his cock hard into her warm, very obliging vagina. She cried out in a mix of pleasure and pain.

Hours later, when their particularly athletic exertions were done, Raquel lay on her side with Duncan's right arm curled over her waist. Having claimed ownership of her physicality, he was already sound asleep, and she was trying hard to achieve the same. The ache she felt in her heart for Phil Proctor, had eased a little. But Duncan was a strange, intense beast indeed.

****

She sat down at her kitchen bench, idly flicking through a two-year-old home improvement magazine. After a while, she picked up the coffee mug beside her and took a sip. She was so engrossed in her 'me' time, that she did not hear Duncan eventually come into the kitchen and stand right next to her. She turned her head when she saw his hand resting on the bench and nearly fell off her stool.

"You frightened me," she smiled up at him.

"Sorry, I didn't mean to. I had some news," he announced, looking quite solemn behind his glasses. He was bare chested, but wearing tan trousers and brown shoes, so she knew he was on the move very soon.

"What's up?"

"I don't know what to think…but work called me a few minutes ago. Someone's found a burnt-out vehicle out in the scrub, about fifty kilometres out from Brumby Flat."

Raquel raised her eyebrows, "Isn't that more like police work? Is it a stolen car?" she asked.

"Yeah, but I have to go and look it over. There's more to it. They believe it's my parents' old Kombi van. Did I tell you the story? My parents, well, they disappeared when I was very young. I was raised by my grandparents."

He looked down and leaned heavily against the kitchen bench.

"Phil," she put her hand over his right hand and squeezed it gently, "I remember you told me."

"I don't know if I am ready to find out…" his voice trailed off and she saw the very apparent deep heartache in his blue eyes when he lifted them, "what exactly happened to them. You know? I wanted this day to come but then, maybe not. I'm not sure what to feel."

She nodded her head, tears welling in the corners of her eyes. She understood that it would be very hard for him.

"I'd better go. I'll be back as soon as I can," he bent over and kissed her forehead gently. He made the tender gesture seem so natural, as if he had kissed her every morning in that way for the longest time.

Cradling her coffee mug carefully in both hands, she followed him to the front door as he struggled into his shirt, buttoned it and walked out. He carried his tie out with him. A stray tear streamed down her right cheek as she watched him get into his white station wagon and drive away.

Their future had started with some promise. She dearly hoped that Bette was looking down and forgiving of her. After all, she had not approached Phillip Duncan. It was Duncan who had come to her.

To be continued in the final book of the trilogy
'Drop Dead Like Flies'